W9-CGR-198

Getaway

I Found My Heart in San Francisco Book Seven

To KAREN-
ALL THE BEST!
Susan X Meagher

Susan X Meagher

GETAWAY

I FOUND MY HEART IN SAN FRANCISCO: BOOK SEVEN

ISBN-10 09799254-0-1
ISBN-13 978-0-9799254-0-5

THIS TRADE PAPERBACK ORIGINAL IS PUBLISHED BY BRISK PRESS, NEW YORK, NY 10011

COVER DESIGN BY CAROLYN NORMAN

FIRST PRINTING: OCTOBER 2007

By Susan X Meagher

Novels

Cherry Grove

All That Matters

Arbor Vitae

Serial Novels

I Found My Heart in San Francisco:

Awakenings

Beginnings

Coalescence

Disclosures

Entwined

Fidelity

Getaway

Anthologies

Girl Meets Girl

Tales of Travelrotica for Lesbians: Vol 2

Undercover Tales

Telltale Kisses

The Milk of Human Kindness

Infinite Pleasures

Acknowledgments

Thanks to Karen for her help in editing these stories.

Dedication

For the love of my life, for the rest of my life.

Chapter One

A little past seven on a bright, cool August morning, Catherine Evans walked down the long hall of the second floor of her home, eagerly anticipating beginning her day. Her usual waking hour was around nine, but she was so excited to have Jamie, Ryan, and little Caitlin visiting that she found herself wide awake just after the sun rose.

She had showered and was fully dressed in what was, for her, a very casual outfit—navy blue cotton slacks and a mint green cotton blouse, the long sleeves rolled up a few times. Approaching the door to Jamie's old nursery, she pressed her ear to the door to determine if the baby was already awake. When she heard nothing, she opened the door stealthily and blinked in surprise to see that the crib was empty. *Oh...the girls must have taken her into their bed. I hope she didn't keep them up all night. Ryan looked absolutely exhausted yesterday and she's going to need to be well rested to enjoy our trip.*

The soft sounds of inchoate speech caught her attention, and she walked to the door that joined the nursery to Jamie's room. Poking her head in just a few inches, she had to stifle a laugh at the scene that was playing out on the bed. Ryan was lying on her back, a pillow pressed over her face and held in place by one long, bare arm. Jamie was cuddled up against her right side, arms and legs haphazardly entwined with her partner. A bright blonde head peeked out from between their merged bodies, the baby reclining against Ryan's torso, her little feet rhythmically kneading Jamie's belly. She was fully awake, seemingly quite content to lie in her little nest as she sang an atonal song of her own creation.

Catherine was about to back out of the room when the baby caught sight of her. Immediately the contented little song turned into a grunt of dismay as the little pea struggled to extricate herself from her pod.

Averting her eyes from what she assumed were nude bodies under the sheet, Catherine crept over to the bed and held her hands out to the grasping infant. The sunny smile that immediately suffused Caitlin's face filled Catherine with joy and the two blondes cuddled each other for a moment. No sooner had Catherine taken a step with the baby than the pillow was shoved away from Ryan's face and the dark head lifted in confusion, her expression comically stunned. Placing her hand on Ryan's shoulder, Catherine said softly, "Go back to sleep, dear. I can keep her occupied for a while."

With a massive sigh, Ryan fell back to the mattress, muttering, "I worship you," her eyes closing once again. Obviously missing the full-body contact, Jamie snuggled closer to Ryan, mumbling something in her sleep while she wrapped her hand tightly around Ryan's shoulder, effectively trapping her.

Shaking her head in amusement, Catherine carried the baby from the room, the little blonde head swiveling just a bit to see if the rest of the gang would join them. To Catherine's great pleasure, Caitlin accepted their decision to sit this one out and focused her attention on the thin gold chain that Catherine had made the mistake of wearing. The twosome walked down to the sunny kitchen, ready to start the day. *Now if only one of us knew how to make breakfast*, Catherine mused, deciding that it was never too late—nor too early—to learn.

When Ryan entered the kitchen two hours later, she was a little surprised at the mess but quite pleased to see several plates with remnants of adult and baby food. *It's good to know that Catherine isn't so helpless after all*, she mused. *Unless she borrowed one of the neighbors' cooks…*

She could hear Caitlin's delighted laughter from somewhere in the back yard and went in search of the pair, finding them playing in the formal gardens behind the pool. Catherine was introducing Caitlin to the great variety of flowers in the well-tended space, holding her little face above the various plants and allowing her to sniff the multitude of aromas. Caitlin seemed to be enjoying herself, continually looking to Catherine to mimic her actions.

Ryan left the hiding place from which she had been observing the two, and when her feet hit the gravel pathway, Caitlin screamed in delight and held out her little arms to go to her cousin. "How can you ever be in a bad mood when someone is so happy to see you in the morning?" Ryan asked rhetorically, sharing a dazzling smile with the baby.

Caitlin cuddled up to her contentedly, nuzzling against Ryan's warm body for a few minutes while Catherine looked on. "I don't think I've ever had a more enjoyable morning," Catherine mused while watching the cousins reconnect. "It's impossible not to see the world through new eyes when you have such an inquisitive little soul in your arms."

"Isn't that the truth? I learn something every time I'm with her."

"Would you like some breakfast? I made a large serving of the world's most expensive oatmeal while you two slept."

"Most expensive…?"

"Well, the oatmeal wasn't expensive," Catherine allowed. "But the 45-minute call to Spain certainly helped drive up the cost."

"Spain?"

"Marta's with her family in Spain this month. Luckily, she's a very patient woman, and she didn't mind telling me where everything was located and walking me through the process. I'm not sure I made the oatmeal correctly, but Caitlin and I both rather enjoyed it."

"You're wearing a good bit of it," Ryan observed, picking a hunk of the congealed cereal from Catherine's hair.

"That's where that last spoonful went! I looked all over for that. When Caitlin gets a spoon in her hand it's best to take cover."

Ryan pushed back from the table, her mood bright and her stomach pleasantly full. "I don't know about the rest of you, but nothing would feel better to me than a nice swim."

"Not for me, but I'm sure Caitlin would accompany you," Jamie said. "After you two play for a while, we can go home and get packed for the trip. I suppose we should sleep here again, then we can all go to the airport together tomorrow."

"That's fine. I think Caitie slept well here, and it was nice to have a real room for her. I think she does better when she can't lie in her crib and watch us all night." Realizing how that sounded, she hastened to add, "You know, she stays in her crib and plays quietly in the morning if she has her own room."

"Yes, dear," Jamie smirked, catching the grin her mother tried to stifle. "We knew exactly what you meant."

Rolling her eyes, Ryan got to her feet, stretched languidly for a moment, but stopped short when she realized, "I don't have a suit."

"Neither does Caitlin, and that didn't stop her," Jamie said, batting her eyes at her partner. Ryan continued to gaze at Jamie, not saying a word, a patient smile on her face. "Okay," Jamie said, chuckling, "you can wear one of mine. Second drawer, left hand side of my dresser."

"Be right back."

"I don't think Ryan will get much swimming in if Caitlin is with her," Jamie said, "but she had more than enough activity at her training camp. I wish she would just take it easy for a few days, but trying to convince her of that is like talking to a wall."

"She does seem to have a determined personality," Catherine agreed. "I'm surprised that you don't fight more. You're not exactly a pushover either."

Acknowledging the truth of the statement, Jamie nodded contemplatively. "It's funny that we don't fight much. I suppose it's because neither of us tries to change the other. I mean, I really want Ryan to relax and lie in a lounge chair all day, but I know she won't. I try not to bug her to get her to do what I want—mainly because I know it won't work. Of course, that doesn't mean that I won't try to talk her into a nice long nap later." She grinned impishly. "I just have to use the right enticements."

"Did someone say enticements?" Ryan asked, popping her head around the corner.

"Yes, love. I was just telling mother that I was going to entice you to take a nap with me later."

Entering the room, Ryan strode across the floor and picked Caitlin up from Jamie's embrace. "That won't be a tough sell. I'm really dragging today."

"Didn't you sleep well?" Catherine asked.

"I slept well, just not long enough. Caitlin woke me three times, and I spent almost an hour with her at around four."

"I didn't know that!" Jamie exclaimed. "I thought she slept through the night."

"That's because *you* slept through the night," Ryan said, tweaking her partner's nose. "Come on, Little Bits," she said to Caitlin, "let's go swimming."

"Did you find a suit?" Jamie asked, gazing at Ryan's outfit—the same one she had left in.

"Yeah, but I didn't have anything to put on over it. Your robes were all too small."

"It's okay. You don't have to be modest here. It's just us girls." Surveying Ryan's rumpled clothes, Jamie offered, "Give me your clothes, and I'll wash them and Caitlin's dress while you play."

"You sure?" she asked, casting a hesitant look in Catherine's direction.

"Sure. Hand 'em over."

Sensing that Ryan was uncomfortable undressing in front of her, Catherine stood and announced, "I'm going to go to my office and start making some phone calls about our trip. I'll be there if you need me."

As Catherine left the room, Ryan returned Caitlin to Jamie and quickly dropped her slacks to the floor. Jamie's eyes grew in size as the buttons on Ryan's blouse opened, revealing a dazzling display of womanly pulchritude. Jamie blinked as she slowly trailed around her partner, a low, soft whistle escaping from her lips. "My Lord, Ryan! How did you manage to even get that on?"

The microscopic bikini that Ryan wore was at least three sizes too small for her, but Jamie was the last person on earth to complain. The bandeau top strained to contain her full breasts, creamy flesh spilling over the top of the bright blue fabric. It truly looked as though one deep breath would rend the material, and Jamie fought with her conscience to stop herself from poking Ryan in the stomach to elicit the gasp she hoped for. The tiny bottoms weren't much more successful at reining in the bounty, and Ryan's smooth cheeks protruded from the fabric in a nearly scandalous fashion.

"This was the best of the bunch." She blushed girlishly, turning her head to look over her shoulder. "The other ones were one-pieces, and they were so short I couldn't stand up straight."

"You know, you'd look less tantalizing if you went swimming in the buff." At Ryan's slightly perturbed glance, Jamie hastened to add, "Don't get me wrong, you're fantastic naked—it's just that this tiny little suit makes it look like you're intentionally showing off your wares." She ran her thumb over Ryan's firm nipple, giving her a sexy smile as she did so. "Please don't take that as a criticism. You can show off any old time for me."

"Never mind," Ryan grumbled, turning to go back upstairs. "We can just go back home and pack."

"No way, love," Jamie insisted, placing a restraining hand on her arm. "Take that little thing off before you cut off the blood flow to some vital part, and get out there. Mother will be in her office, which doesn't face the pool. I'll tell her that you need a little privacy. No big deal."

"You sure?" Ryan looked conflicted, but it was clear she wanted to accept the offer.

"Positive. Now scoot."

Without another word, the suit was peeled off, Jamie's mouth watering when Ryan's breasts jiggled as they were set free. "Maybe we should take that nap now," the entranced woman murmured, leaning forward to wrap her lips around one hard nipple.

"Swim first," Ryan said, pulling away with a "pop" as she broke the suction of Jamie's hungry mouth. "Keep that thought," she said, patting her partner's cheek as she ran into the yard with Caitlin in her arms, both swimmers shouting for joy.

Having a built-in excuse, the two cousins stayed in the pool until Jamie came out to announce that their clothes were washed, dried and ironed. "This is the life, eh Cait?" Ryan asked conspiratorially as she carried the gurgling baby to the steps. "What's that you say? Oh...I guess this is the treatment you're used to, isn't it?" Looking at Jamie, Ryan shrugged her shoulders and said, "Caitie says you're gonna have to work a little harder to impress her. I, however, think you're fantastic."

"Thank you. I think you're both fantastic, too. Ready for a shower? I waited for you."

"Uhm, sure, but can I go in the house in just a towel?"

"Sure. But you don't have to. Let's shower in the pool house. I'll bring your clothes in."

"You have a shower in there?" Ryan asked, gazing at the neat square, two-story house that stood perpendicular to the main house.

"Yep. A really nice one," Jamie informed her interested partner.

"My sweet Lord!" Ryan exclaimed, purring sensually as the warm water cascaded down her body. "I have never been in a shower that felt better than this. Can we move here?" Before the words were fully out of her mouth, she grimly reminded herself that Jim would probably not be wild about that idea, and that she needed to tell Jamie about his visit as soon as possible.

"Sure. It would be a tough commute to school, but if it would make you happy—we're here."

"I guess this is better as a getaway than as a full-time residence," Ryan decided, knowing that Hillsborough was too far from home even if Jim didn't hate her.

Jamie was holding Caitlin, who was having as good a time as her big cousin. The waterfall-style showerhead propelled a foot-wide stream of water onto their heads, and the baby laughed while she sputtered and spit, trying to get the water out of her eyes. Taking pity on her, Jamie moved back in the stall, where she immediately shot a puzzled glance down at her leg.

Ryan saw the look on Caitlin's face and knew that she was relieving herself on Jamie's leg, but she wasn't about to break the news if Jamie didn't notice it. Regrettably, Jamie caught her in mid-stream, making a disgusted face as she grasped the baby and held her at arm's length. "Gross!" she cried, maintaining her sour face.

Please don't add any solids, Caitlin, Ryan pleaded, wisely keeping that thought to herself. "Does this mean that you won't indulge in my fetish for golden showers?"

"I'm not absolutely certain what that means, but given the context, I'd say that's a resounding no."

"You're no fun."

"Speaking of fun," Jamie asked, "what do you want to do with munchkin the rest of the day? Should we take her back to the city with us?"

"Well, if I had my choice, I'd like to cut her hair. She looks like a nut with this goofy haircut, and I've been itching to get my hands on it for months. Annie gave me carte blanche to do anything I want, including shaving her head."

Jamie pretended to be considering that option. "I don't think that would flatter her," she decided, "but she does need some help."

Getting out and drying off, Jamie tried to slide a wide-toothed comb through the baby's wet locks, which featured at least 16 different lengths. The very fine hair on the back of her head was short, but permanently tangled from sleeping on her back, and it was clear that Annie had declared the area a total loss. Very long strands of golden hair grew from the crown of her head. They were not bad looking, but they were uneven and they blew around Caitlin's head in the smallest breeze. The worst part of the cut, however, were the very short, annoyingly uneven bangs that zigged and zagged haphazardly across her forehead, looking more like they had been chewed than cut.

"Da has a set of clippers at the house," Ryan suggested, seemingly in earnest.

Jamie's eyes grew round as saucers, as she stared at her partner in horror. "Absolutely not. Neither of us knows how to cut hair with clippers, and I will not have this adorable child look *worse* when we've finished with her."

Ryan scratched her head pensively. "I don't think she could look worse."

"Ryan, the child needs a good haircut, and she's going to get one." With that, the determined woman strode across the pool deck, baby in her arms.

I do believe this is one of those, "Give up, and follow orders" kinda days, Ryan mused.

Ryan sat at the kitchen table, watching her partner make arrangements to take Caitlin to Giancarlo for her first official haircut. "Three o'clock is fine," she said into the phone. "No, just a cut. Great. See you then." Turning to Ryan, she announced, "Let's go home, get packed up and then head over to Berkeley."

"Okay. Let's go tell your mom."

Catherine was pleased with the plan, and she offered to take the baby separately so that Jamie and Ryan could get packed up more efficiently. That settled, Ryan decided that she needed a little lunch, so they repaired to the kitchen for the noon meal. The day was getting away from Ryan, and she knew that she had to talk to Jamie, but she found herself trying to think of any reason to delay. Deciding that she was just making matters worse by waiting, she sat down at the table with the baby and cleared her throat. "Uhm…Jamie?" she said, getting a questioning glance from both mother and daughter. "I mentioned this to your mom last night when you were gone, but I've been putting off telling you something."

"What is it?" Jamie focused her attention on her partner and pulled her chair up next to her.

Taking a gulp of air, Ryan said, "The morning that you left for Rhode Island, your dad came to our house in Berkeley."

The mere start of the story caused Jamie to clench her fists, her mouth a grim line. She said nothing, but it was clear that she was expecting the worst.

"We had words," Ryan said, cutting to the chase. "Mostly about money, of course. The uhm…bottom line is that he told me that I had to move out."

Catherine cast a worried glance at her daughter as the young woman rose from the table, muttering a tense, "I'll be back," before stalking out of the room.

Ryan sighed heavily, shaking her head as she watched her partner depart. "Well, that went well."

"Why did she leave?" Catherine asked.

"She doesn't like to yell at me, so when she's really angry she likes to be alone to blow off some steam. I guess she also didn't want to start hollering in front of Caitlin."

"But why is she angry with you?"

"Because I didn't tell her when it happened," Ryan said, having known the entire time that she was doing something that would hurt her lover. "She hates to be treated like a child."

"She always did," Catherine mused thoughtfully, "even when she was one." She looked out the large window, just able to make out her daughter's shape in the distance. "You know, Ryan, I think that's one of the reasons that I never took her to places like Disneyland. She never seemed like she would enjoy those child-centered places. Even at Caitlin's age, she was rather serious and quite somber."

Ryan sighed again, realizing that she had made a mistake in trying to control the flow of information that her partner received. "I think I'll go find her to apologize."

"She's on the tennis court," Catherine hazarded, even though she couldn't see the court from where she sat. "That's where she's always gone to deal with her frustrations."

As predicted, Jamie was trying to smash the covers off the fluorescent green balls that the electric ball machine shot at her. Sensing rather than seeing Ryan, she growled, "You'd better give me some time. I'm not responsible for my mouth right now."

Ignoring the warning, Ryan continued on her course, quietly sitting down on the court behind her partner. A few minutes passed as she watched Jamie whip the balls down the line. "How about if I talk for a minute," she suggested. "I came to apologize. I know that what I did was wrong, and I want you to know that I'm really sorry."

"Do you know why I'm angry?" The question was forced through gritted teeth.

"I think so. I think you're angry because I tried to think for you."

"Ace," Jamie grunted, apparently in reply to Ryan's answer.

"I tried to figure out the best time to tell you what happened instead of just telling you when I talked to you. I think you're mad because it really pisses you off to have me, or anyone else, keep you in the dark about something—especially something like this."

"That's about it," Jamie snapped. "Good answer for somebody that obviously didn't realize that just last Sunday."

Her derisive tone stung, and Ryan took a breath to control herself from snapping off a sharp rejoinder. "I said I'm sorry. I'll try never to do that to you again." She pushed herself up, walking dejectedly to the opening in the fence that surrounded the court. "I can't do any better than that."

She quietly closed the gate and had traveled about 15 feet when she heard her partner's rapid footsteps scampering across the court's surface. "Ryan, wait! Please," she called, flinging the gate open.

Ryan paused, waiting patiently but not turning. Soon she felt Jamie's damp hand on her own, and she turned to face her flushed partner. "I'm sorry, too. I know that you must have had a good reason for keeping this from me."

"I'm not sure that I did," Ryan admitted. "I think part of the reason that I didn't tell you was because I just didn't want to deal with it. I was down in my little isolated cocoon, and I was able to put it aside by not talking about it. I couldn't have done that if you were all upset about it."

Snaking an arm around Ryan's waist, Jamie laid her head against the warm chest that was presented when Ryan raised her arm. "That's a pretty good reason, in my book. I know last week was hard for you. I'm sure you did the best you could."

"I tried to, Jamie," Ryan whispered, placing soft kisses on the top of her head. "But I'll admit to being a chicken," she said, her voice low and soft. "I just felt so odd and unstable being locked away down in Santa Cruz that I really went out of my way to keep things calm. I'm sorry I screwed up."

"It's okay. Let me turn off the ball machine, and we can go back inside."

Ryan gave her a firm squeeze and said, "Thanks for being so understanding about this."

"You did your best…you always do."

The rest of the discussion went very well now that Jamie was no longer angry. Catherine reaffirmed that the house was in her name alone, and that she would not allow Jim to dictate who was allowed to live there. Jamie wasn't very happy with that, not wanting her mother to be put in the middle, but since she didn't see many options she agreed.

"I don't think this is going to place me any higher on Jim's favorites list," Ryan groused, knowing that the powerful attorney was not the kind of guy she wanted to have angry with her.

"He's just having a tantrum," Catherine said. "This will all blow over quickly, Ryan. Don't give it another thought."

Wouldn't that be nice? Ryan thought, knowing that Jim was not so easily dismissed.

At three o'clock, Jamie stood in the doorway of Giancarlo's salon, peering down the street, looking for her mother and Caitlin. She spotted the pair nearly running down the street, Catherine clutching the baby in one arm and several shopping bags in the other.

Handing the baby to her daughter, Catherine panted, "I've got to put some money in the parking meter. Be back in a few." With that she was gone, heading in the direction whence she had come, at nearly the same pace. Ryan approached from the other direction, having spent the previous 15 minutes looking for an ever-elusive parking meter.

Seeing Jamie enter, Carlo immediately came over to them and began to make over the baby in the most excessive fashion that either woman had ever witnessed. After a few moments of admiring the child shyly nestled in Jamie's arms, Carlo shot an admiring glance at Ryan. "How did you do this?" he demanded, his hands on his hips. "Jamie tells me how talented you are, but this..." he indicated the baby, "is too, too much!" He turned to Jamie and said something in Italian that had her nearly in stitches. She replied with a comment that had him howling with laughter as he snatched the baby from her and took her over to the sink to wash her hair.

"Okay," Jamie said as she leaned in close to her lover. "I promised I'd try to keep you in the conversation, so here goes. I'm not sure that I can do it, but I'm gonna try to translate this so it has the same punch." She took a deep breath, furrowing her brow a bit as she struggled to find an appropriate translation. "Carlo asked if you were a...gorgeous transvestite or an extremely talented lesbian who could produce a baby by the...uhm...skillful use of your tongue."

Ryan rolled her eyes as a deep blush crawled up her neck. "Wha...what did you say?" she stammered.

"I said," Jamie replied as she got even closer to Ryan's bent head, "that I had explored every inch of your precious body and that I could assure him that you were a gorgeous, talented lesbian who could in fact do marvelous things with your tongue, but producing a baby was not one of them."

Ryan pulled her head back as she stared at her lover for a moment in stunned silence. "Honey," she finally said as she slid an arm around her shoulders, "don't bother to translate any more. I kind of like being kept in the dark."

With Ryan still shaking her head, they walked over to where Carlo had set up shop with Caitlin. Much to the baby's pleasure, he had stripped her completely naked and placed her in the deep sink used for hair washing. She held a short comb in each hand and was splashing around happily in the few inches of water that he had drawn. He looked over at Jamie and stated proudly, "The baby, she likes, no?"

"She likes water very much, Carlo. Excellent idea."

He washed her hair with a minimum of fuss and not too much splashing due to the depth of the sink. Jamie came over with a smock that she insisted Carlo put on after she saw one too many water droplets hit his Armani slacks. Since things were going so well, he decided to cut her hair while she sat in the sink. Caitlin was very much in favor of this, as she giggled and splashed in her makeshift tub. Ryan sorted through the backpack she had brought, and she found some plastic toys that the baby was particularly fond of. Now Caitie was really in heaven, and she barely noticed that a stranger was carefully assessing her hair.

Carlo muttered to himself for a few minutes as he got a complete look at her current hairdo. He finally could not contain his wrath as he turned to Jamie, his nearly black eyes flashing as he demanded, "Who put the baby's head in the fan?"

"What?" Jamie asked, completely confused, assuming that Carlo must have mistranslated something.

"Nothing else would explain this....this..." he fumed as he held up the longest locks, "butchering!"

"Her mother has a hard time keeping her still," Jamie explained weakly as she watched Caitlin play placidly in the tub, looking like the calmest baby on earth.

Crossing his muscular arms over his chest, he turned slowly and cast a baleful glance at the tranquil child. He obviously decided that his point had been made since he did not continue his rant. Instead, he began to sing a delightful, lilting melody that included little tickles and much splashing of water. He worked very quickly, but with a sureness of vision that was unwavering. In less than ten minutes the cut was finished, and all agreed that it was absolute perfection. Now Caitlin's hair was a perfect one-inch long all over her head. The delicate golden locks framed her face and made her look positively angelic. Carlo drained the water and took the hand held sprayer and carefully rinsed all of the hair off her chubby little body, then he wrapped her up in a big fluffy towel and handed her to Jamie. "Sit," he ordered as he guided the twosome to a chair. He produced his dryer, equipped with a diffuser, and very gently blew the new style dry in a matter of moments.

Both Ryan and Jamie were astounded at the transformation. The cut was perfect for Caitlin's sweet little face, surrounding her beatific features like a gilt frame.

Catherine entered the shop just as Carlo finished drying the baby's hair. She gasped in delight, saying, "You are an absolute artist!"

"Carlo, this is my mother, Catherine," Jamie said. "Mother, this is Giancarlo, whom you've been hearing me praise for three years now."

Slipping into her lightly accented Italian, Catherine proceeded to charm the easily charmed man all the way down to his Gucci loafers. They bantered back and forth for a few moments, complimenting each other on their clothing and their favorite restaurants, and agreeing on the superiority of all things Italian. A client was sitting in the waiting area, looking pointedly at her watch, and Jamie caught her mother's eye, indicating that they should leave.

"No, no, stay for a drink," Carlo insisted.

"But Carlo, you have another client," Jamie reminded him, as discreetly as possible.

He cast a quick glance at the woman, who now looked completely perturbed with him. Marching over to her, he pointed at his watch, at the assembled women gathered near his station, once again at his watch, and after a dramatic shrug of his shoulders, the woman's face grew red and she stormed out of the shop.

"Arrivederci," he muttered, adding a dismissive wave of his hand as he walked back to the group. "Now, who would like a drink?"

Glancing at her watch, Catherine said, "A little Campari?"

"But of course!" he said, seemingly never having heard of a better idea.

Over drinks for Catherine and Giancarlo, a bottle for Caitlin, and glasses of San Pellegrino for Jamie and Ryan, Catherine broached the subject of her own hair. "Carlo, I think I'm ready to make a change with my hair. What do you think?"

"I think I will make the Botticelli's Venus weep with envy," he confidently declared, taking Catherine's hand in his.

Thirty minutes later, three sets of critical, and one pair of vaguely interested eyes assessed Giancarlo's creation. Catherine, Jamie, and Ryan all agreed that it was the cut that was designed for Catherine's face, and Caitlin offered no objection, so they were essentially unanimous. In effect, the cut was a slightly longer version of Caitlin's, with just a bit more length on the top and a little more tapering near the nape of her neck.

As Ryan took another step back to look at the style, she mused that when she'd first met Catherine, she had decided that the only element of her polished image that didn't work to perfection was her haircut. This new, more modern style was the antidote to that one flaw, and Ryan considered that Catherine now could easily pass for Jamie's older sister. "It's absolutely perfect," she said appreciatively, smiling broadly at Giancarlo.

"Thank you, thank you," he said, sketching a bow. "I follow Michelangelo's theory, you know."

"Ah…no, I didn't know that. How so?"

"I study the face and the personality of the woman, and then I take away all of the hair that does not belong," he explained, quite proud of himself. "Now that your mother looks even more beautiful, it's your turn, Jamie," he said as he turned his attention to the younger Evans woman.

"I know I need a cut, but do you have time?"

"For you? Anything, cara mia. You've brought me such joy today that I should cut your hair for free." His face broke into a charming grin as he added, "But I will not!"

Ryan was sent for more sparkling water, and she decided to take Caitlin along for the walk. When they returned, Jamie was just finishing up, and Carlo looked at Ryan and said, "Come on, lover girl, you're next."

"Me?" she asked, jerking a thumb at herself.

"Yes, you," he said with his hands on his hips. "Jamie, please explain to the beautiful one that hair grows. It must be cut to maintain the perfection of my creation."

Ryan cast a helpless glance at Jamie, but she just shrugged her shoulders in reply, knowing that Carlo would eventually win the argument. After a quick shampoo, Carlo set about removing no more than an eighth of an inch from his creation. Ryan ventured a suggestion that he cut her bangs a bit, but he sternly informed her that she was not allowed to have bangs any longer. He turned to Jamie and explained carefully with a lavish degree of hand gesturing why he would no longer allow the offending wisps of hair, and she nodded in agreement. The dialogue had gone on for at least three or four minutes, but when Jamie turned to Ryan she merely shrugged her shoulders and said, "No more bangs."

Rolling her eyes dramatically, Ryan wisely kept her opinion to herself, reasoning that Jamie really did seem to prefer her hair blown back from her face, and that was really all that mattered.

When they were all finished, Jamie went to settle the bill while Carlo carried Caitlin around the shop, introducing her to every other patron and stylist. She was having a ball and giggled nonstop as she met each person. She was snuggled up against Giancarlo as though she had known him all of her short life, and when Jamie returned, she was none too happy to leave his warm embrace.

Her happy little face turned to a sad grimace as they tried to put her back into her baby sling, and Carlo insisted on taking her back into his arms. "You don't want to leave Carlo, do you?" he crooned. As long as she was wrapped in his toned, tanned arms, the baby was the picture of bliss. Turning to Jamie he ordered, "You must bring her in at least once a month. She is magnifica! And she loves me. See?" he demanded as the baby cuddled and batted her eyes at him shamelessly.

"She certainly does," Jamie admitted. "I suppose we'll just have to bring her over, Carlo."

He sidled up to Ryan, asking, "Why don't you have your brother bring the baby when he returns?"

"Ah, my brother isn't gay, Carlo," Ryan informed him, surprised that Conor hadn't made a point of his sexual orientation.

He blinked his dark eyes at her, cocking his head slightly in question. "This affects me, how?"

Ryan blushed deeply, obviously misinterpreting Carlo's intentions. "Oh! I thought you were..."

"Very short hair must be cut more often, beautiful one. Your brother and Caitlin need their hair cut every month. You, however, can come four times a year. Since he must come more often, he should bring the baby. What of that don't you understand?"

"I understand perfectly, Carlo," she said, still blushing.

"Lesbians," he scoffed. "Always with the sex...sex...sex on their minds!"

After a tearful goodbye, the foursome left Giancarlo. Catherine wanted to do a little more shopping and she had the car seat, so she suggested that she'd take Caitlin with her. Jamie offered to stop at the store to pick up dinner, and she and Ryan watched Catherine walk away, without a peep of displeasure from the child.

"Boy, Caitlin is just crazy about your mom. I've never seen her this happy to be with a stranger."

"How many strangers is she ever around?" Jamie asked, smirking, knowing that the Driscolls and the O'Flahertys took up most of Caitlin's social calendar.

"Good point." Deciding to get another bit of business out of the way she added, "Come to think of it, she warmed up to another stranger yesterday."

"Really? You mentioned you took Caitlin out to lunch. Is that what you mean?"

Boy, she never misses a thing, Ryan thought glumly. *She might not tell me she caught something, but she stores it all away up in that cute little head.* "Yep. Caitlin and I were at Mass yesterday, and Sara came in and joined us." She saw a twitch in Jamie's cheek but her face otherwise remained impassive.

"So you had lunch together?"

"Yeah. We had lunch, and I told her all about everything I'd found out about what happened to me in high school. Caitlin really took to her, too," she said lightly. "Maybe she does prefer strangers."

"Anything else?" Jamie asked with studied casualness as Ryan again felt the weight of her prescience.

"Yes," she replied, looking down at the ground. "I told her I didn't want to see her alone anymore. I said I would like to get to know her again, but only when you and I are together."

Jamie stopped in her tracks and stared at Ryan for a long while. "Why?" she asked simply, staring into her eyes.

Ryan pursed her lips and shifted her gaze to stare blankly across the street for a long moment. Finally, she said, "Two reasons. One—I know it bothers you, and it's not something that means enough to me to risk hurting you over. Two—I realized yesterday that I don't have a relationship with her. Everything we have is from seven years ago. When I'm with her, I keep imagining that we're both like we were then, but we're not that way any longer, so it's not like a real relationship. And if I'm going to build a new relationship with her, I want you to be involved too."

Jamie nodded her head, but the mere set of her posture told Ryan that she didn't buy that explanation. She looked up at Ryan and said, "It's too painful…and too tempting, isn't it?" Her eyes bored into Ryan's, compelling her to admit the whole truth.

Ryan closed her eyes and nodded. She was moved deeply by Jamie's thorough knowledge of her inner self, but this knowledge also left her feeling very vulnerable and exposed. It was both reassuring and terribly uncomfortable, and she was sure that duality showed on her face. "I told Sara how sorry I was that I had hurt you," she explained with a pained look on her face. "I explained that I'd never put myself in another compromising position with her, and that precluded spending time with her alone. I wanted her to understand that my love for you is the most important thing to me, and that I would never do anything to make you doubt me again."

Jamie looked at the open, trusting expression on her partner's face for a long time, finding herself reassured that the entire truth was out in the open. She opened her arms and Ryan buried her head in her shoulder, soaking up the comfort as quickly as Jamie could offer it. "Thank you, baby," she whispered. "Thank you for knowing how much it hurt me when you kissed her, and for doing what you have to do to make sure it never happens again. It means so much to me to be taken seriously."

Ryan lifted her head and said, "I do take you seriously. And I take our relationship seriously. That's why I went a little further and told her some things that were pretty hard for her to hear."

They started walking again, Jamie confident that Ryan would tell all at her own pace. They had only traveled a few feet when she revealed quietly, "She asked me if I love you more than I loved her."

Jamie could feel her heart stop beating as her stomach revolted and caused her to feel a wave of nausea. She gripped Ryan's hand harder than she should have, blinking at the startled cry her partner let out.

Ryan stopped and grasped her by the shoulders, turning her so that they stood face to face. "I told her that I couldn't compare my feelings. I think it diminishes love to rate it or compare it. But I also told her that I'd choose you in a heartbeat if given the choice."

"Why did you say that?" she gasped. "That must have hurt her badly."

"I felt like I needed to be honest. It's unfair to both of us to have this thing between us."

"What do you mean by 'thing'?" she asked, confused.

"It's complex," Ryan admitted, releasing Jamie's shoulders and starting to walk again. "I think we both feel that if things had worked out differently that year, we'd still be together."

Jamie sucked in a breath, blinking slowly, trying to figure out where Ryan was going with this train of thought.

"But things didn't go well, and we never got the chance to see how we would do as lovers. Now, I might be wrong, but I got the impression that Sara thinks that if you and I broke up, she and I would get back together and live happily ever after."

"You don't think that?" Jamie asked slowly, feeling in her heart that was exactly what would happen.

"No, I don't." The sadness that often colored her expression when she spoke of Sara was evident as Ryan continued, "Sara did some things that showed me who she really is. Some of those things are understandable and forgivable, but some aren't. I honestly don't think that I could ever trust her again."

"Really?" Jamie gasped. "I…why?"

"She claims she's loved me all this time, right? But she's been out of her parents' house for all those years and never called, never wrote, and never tried to get in contact with me. She didn't contact me because she thought I'd be angry, and it wasn't worth it to risk my wrath. What kind of love is that? Jesus!"

Ryan was clearly frustrated, but Jamie wasn't sure what was troubling her. "Here's the rub," she said earnestly. "If I had never met you, I would have given Sara another chance. I don't think I would have known what real love was, and I would have settled for what she was able to offer me. But now that I've known you, and know what real love is, I honestly don't think Sara and I would have had a chance."

Jamie was drawn to Ryan's embrace, even though they were on a fairly busy street in Berkeley. They held each other for a few seconds, and Ryan continued to talk. "I mean, look at the facts. You're willing to give up the most important relationship in your life for me. That's what love is, Jamie. It's not just attraction and chemistry. It's being willing to sacrifice and suffer, and I know you'll do that. I thought Sara needed to know that I had no confidence that she would do that for me."

"But why did you need to tell her that? Isn't it enough that you know it?"

"No, it's not," Ryan said, taking Jamie's hand and continuing to walk down the street. She blinked back a few tears and said, "I needed to tell her because I want her to get on with her life. She's stuck in a time warp. The woman hasn't made one significant step forward since that day in 1992. She hasn't even tried to find someone to love, she hasn't come out to anyone...she's living in a fantasy world, Jamie, and I want her to know that it's just that—a fantasy."

"God, that must have hurt her," Jamie whispered, feeling the pain in her gut.

Ryan nodded, acknowledging the truth of the statement. "It did. But I'd rather hurt her than let her continue to delude herself. I love Sara, Jamie, and I always will. I'll do whatever I can to help her get on with her life. I just needed to let her know that, no matter what happens, she and I will never be together."

They walked the rest of the way in silence, their hands linked tightly. When they got to the car, Jamie slid into the passenger seat and asked the one question that still puzzled her. "If you're so confident that you'll never be together, why is it still tempting to be with her?"

Ryan sat quietly, her hands resting in her lap. She was always so active that it looked a little odd to see her so still. "I guess it's the battle between my heart and my head," she finally said. "I know that I could never trust Sara again, and I would never make the choice to be with her because of that. But I'm still attracted to her, Jamie. All of the things that made me fall in love with her are still there. There's a pull that I feel when I'm around her that is just too tempting to play with. It's too evocative, and it reaches that place deep inside that's never fully healed from her betrayal. I wish I didn't feel that way, but I do; and until that attraction dies, I'm not going to take the risk."

Grasping Ryan's hand and pulling it towards her lips, Jamie placed gentle kisses along the knuckles. Her eyes were closed, and she tried to block out the rest of the world and all of her jumbled thoughts and concentrate solely on the warm, strong hand that she held, feeling like her connection to Ryan was the one thing she was sure of. "I wish that you didn't feel that way about her," she said softly, "but I can understand why you told her. It's…it was a very loving gift…for all of us."

"I just want you to know that I choose you, Jamie. Unequivocally. I choose you over everyone else on earth. You are the woman for me," she whispered fervently. "For the rest of my life."

They sat in the still car, on that warm summer evening, wrapped in each other's arms, secure and safe in their love.

Chapter Two

Traffic was utterly abysmal as they inched along on 101 towards Hillsborough. "You know, Caitlin's not the only one who likes being with your mom. I can't tell you how much fun I've had with her. It's funny, but in a way she doesn't seem like your mother. I think Maeve seems more like my mother than Catherine does to you."

"I think I know what you mean," Jamie replied thoughtfully. "I mean, I feel like she's my mother, but our relationship has been more like that of friends for a long time. When I was in high school, things started to change between us. I stopped trying to get mothering from her, and found that we got along much better when we acted like friends."

"Boy, that must have been hard for you. I think that's when I needed my mother the most. There were so many things that I needed guidance on, and I just couldn't get some of it from Da or the boys. Luckily I had Aunt Maeve. That's really when we got a lot closer, you know. I relied on her to help me through some of the rough spots. What did you do when you needed advice?"

"Well, I still had Elizabeth."

Ryan turned and gaped at her, stunned. "You did? I assumed she was long gone by then."

"Oh, no," Jamie said, laughing. "She was still here when I met Jack."

"That's amazing," Ryan said. "What does a nanny do when her little charge is in high school?"

"Not a lot, obviously," Jamie agreed. "But she was part of our family by then." She caught herself and amended her statement a little. "Actually, that's not accurate either. We didn't eat together or do anything together socially. Mother and I went out to dinner most nights, so neither Elizabeth nor Marta had much to do. But Elizabeth didn't really have anywhere else to go. She had family in England but she didn't want to return until her sister was ready to retire. Her sister Gwendolyn was a nanny also, and they wanted to purchase a house together, but her charges were younger than me. So we just kept her on until she was ready to go. She left right before I came to Berkeley."

"Do you miss her?" Ryan asked, not really having a good feeling for how Jamie thought of the woman who had raised her.

"In a way. I mean, she was waiting for me when they brought me home from the hospital. I was with her three times more than I was with my parents. She was a sweet, gentle woman who cared for me very well. But she wasn't my mother, she was an employee, so I never really developed the kind of attachment for her that I might have if we were related. Having a nanny is kind of strange for a child. It takes a while to figure out that they aren't part of your family, but once you do, it's hard to ignore that fact."

"I truly can't imagine that," Ryan admitted. She cast a tentative glance at Jamie as she asked, "Do you want to hire people to help raise our kids?"

"No way! We're raising our kids. But if we have more than one, it might be nice to have an au pair to help out during the day."

"You mean like a college student from another country?"

"Yeah, someone who wanted to study in the U.S. in exchange for room, board and a salary."

"Ooh, like some naïve, sexy little French mademoiselle from the country? That's a great idea," Ryan agreed enthusiastically.

"Or maybe a nice, elderly factory worker from the Ukraine," Jamie suggested, batting her eyes innocently.

"You really know how to take the fun out of a good idea."

"That's what I'm best at, honey," she agreed as she leaned in and gave Ryan a wet kiss on the cheek.

Conor returned Ryan's call as soon as he arrived home from work. "Where are you guys?" he asked, sounding a little grumpy.

"We're down in Hillsborough. Catherine's going to go to Disneyland with us tomorrow, and it made sense to leave from here. Is that a problem?"

"No," he grumbled. "I just thought you'd be here when I got home. I miss you."

God, I'm lucky to have been born into this family, Ryan thought, misting up a little to hear her brother express his feelings. A little impulsively, she asked, "Why don't you come down and have dinner with us? I'm sure Jamie and Caitlin would love to see you."

He paused just a second before he answered. "You sure? Jamie's mom won't mind?"

"I'm sure she won't, but hang on a sec and I'll ask." She placed the phone onto her chest and caught Catherine's attention. "Would you mind if my brother came down for dinner? We've been gone so much, he's feeling a little abandoned."

"Of course not, dear. Does he need me to have someone pick him up?"

Ryan gave her a puzzled look and said, "No, he has a car."

"By all means, Ryan, I'd love to meet him." As Ryan got back on the phone, Catherine wracked her brain, trying to remember who lived at Ryan's house. She knew that she had only brothers, but for the life of her, she couldn't remember how old they were. *He must be younger than Ryan, if he's that needy*, she mused. *Goodness, it must be hard for those children with no parent in the house most of the time. The poor little fellow.*

"Okay, Con," Ryan said. "Catherine is happy to have you. Bring your swimsuit and we can go for a swim after dinner, okay?"

"Cool," he agreed. "Should I bring something? A bottle of wine maybe?"

"Nah, don't bother." She lowered her voice a bit, and said, "What they have lying around here is a lot nicer stuff than we'd ever buy." Thinking of something they had forgotten, she amended, "We could use some ice cream, though. Can you bring some?"

"Sure. No prob."

"One pint should be enough. Jim's not home, so it's just the four of us."

"I know," Conor said. "See you soon."

Huh? How does he know that Jim's not here?

When the doorbell rang an hour later, both Jamie and Ryan were heavily involved in the dinner preparations. "I'll get it," Catherine said, making for the living room.

She opened the door and stepped back, blinking up in shock at the massive hunk of beautifully arranged, testosterone enhanced O'Flaherty. *My God! He's like an Irish version of Michelangelo's David.* Her eyes started at the neatly cut black hair, moving down to the piercing blue eyes, the prominent cheekbones, and the full, sensual lips. The godlike man spoke, his deep voice smooth as honey. "Conor O'Flaherty," he announced, a set of dazzling white teeth revealing themselves.

Struggling with her composure, Catherine extended her hand, feeling the large, warm, callused hand envelop hers. "Catherine Evans," she finally managed, gesturing her guest inside. "Did you have any trouble finding us?"

"No. None at all," Conor assured her. "I've been here before."

"You have?" she blinked, not understanding how that was possible.

"Yes. I drove your husband's Acura up here from Pebble Beach."

So that's how that car got up here, she mused, never having bothered to ask Jim how it had miraculously appeared one day. "Ahh," she said, not wanting to appear as though she didn't know her husband's business. "I must have forgotten. That was very generous of you, Conor."

"Believe me," his smooth voice rumbled, "the pleasure was all mine." His white teeth flashed, his eyes narrowing a bit as he said the word "pleasure."

My God, I feel like a schoolgirl! Get hold of yourself, immediately. The boy can't be more than 25.

Even though Catherine had been married at an early age and had not experienced much before that, she was quite used to male attention. She usually shrugged it off, taking it as a small compliment, but rarely more than that. But this man—this gorgeous younger man—was obviously cognizant of her discomfort, and he was clearly playing with it. She found it both compelling and a little frightening, realizing with a start that he gave off the same kind of energy that Ryan showed around Jamie. *Maybe they're just very friendly people.*

She escorted him into the kitchen, smiling broadly when Caitlin caught sight of him. The baby screamed in delight, crawling across the floor so quickly that she slipped on the smooth stone. Conor stooped, his long body folding gracefully as he swooped the delighted infant into his arms, giving her several dozen kisses as she babbled away, deliriously happy to be in this large, gentle man's arms. "What a cute haircut. She looks like a little doll."

Jamie came over and added a kiss and a hug, ruffling her hand through his newly cropped hair, seemingly very comfortable in Conor's presence. Ryan was stirring something on the stove, and he went to her, still carrying the baby. He wrapped his free arm around his sister, giving her a kiss on the lips as well as a generous hug. *Maybe he* is *just friendly*, Catherine mused. *He certainly does seem well-loved by these three.*

Turning to Catherine, Conor asked, "When is Jim back from Zurich?"

She blinked slowly, trying to recall if she knew that her husband was in Switzerland. "I think he'll be home tomorrow," she said, vaguely recalling the last conversation they had while she was in Newport.

"How do you know where Jim is?" Ryan asked, her eyes narrowing suspiciously.

"Oh, I went to a ball game with him on Friday," he said. "He mentioned that he was leaving the next day. By the way, Jamie, I met your former fiancé that night. He seems like a nice guy."

Jamie blanched, blinking slowly as she took in that bit of information. "You went to a ball game with my father and Jack?"

"Uh-huh." He paused a bit, looking from one shocked face to the next. "Problem?"

"Uhm…no, I guess not," Jamie said, knowing that she had been instrumental in introducing Conor to her father and encouraging the older man to spend some time with him.

Conor was too perceptive to let that weak endorsement satisfy him. He looked to Ryan for further information, cocking his head at his sister. "What's up?"

She pursed her lips, not very happy to reveal the problems they were experiencing with Jim, but feeling that her brother needed to know what was going on, since he was becoming friends with the older man. "We're having some problems with Jim right now, Con. He's not happy with me, and he wants me to move out of Jamie's house."

"What? But how…why?"

"He thinks my motivation for being with Jamie is mostly mercenary," she said softly, not having a better way to characterize Jim's accusations.

"Oh, for Christ's sake!" He got up, and began pacing around the kitchen, Caitlin still cuddled up to his chest. "If either of us wanted his money, it would be me," he said in a rare bit of self-analysis. "I mean, I like him, but if he had a Hyundai I wouldn't have driven it all the way up here from Pebble Beach. I like him because of the stuff he has, but you're not like that."

"I still say that this will blow over," Catherine said. "I think he's just going to take some time to get used to the idea, girls. Once he realizes how serious you are about each other, he'll revert to his normal self."

"I certainly hope so, Mom," Jamie said, not having nearly as much confidence as her mother did.

"Me too," Conor joined in, seeing his dreams of driving nice cars and going to baseball games disintegrate before his very eyes.

After dinner, Conor volunteered to take the baby for her evening swim, since Ryan and Jamie both wanted to avoid washing their hair again. Catherine tried to avert her eyes as much as possible when Conor appeared on the pool deck in his long, brightly colored swim trunks. Even though all of his critical parts were well covered, his stunningly muscular body was much too well displayed for her comfort. The few glances that she allowed herself showed a beautifully built man, his heavy musculature clear evidence of a life spent in manual labor. His skin was a nicely burnished copper, a shade or two darker than his sister's, with his arms, face and neck darker still.

"How old is Conor?" Catherine asked Jamie when Ryan went to fetch ice cream for the group.

"He's 28."

At least I won't be guilty of statutory rape if I throw myself at him, Catherine mused. "You know, Jamie," she said thoughtfully, "if I ever had any doubts about your being gay, they have been completely erased now that I've met Conor."

Jamie laughed heartily, knowing exactly what her mother was getting at. "That would be the litmus test, wouldn't it?"

"I'm afraid your father and I might just have to fight over that young man," Catherine said, laughing.

"Wait 'til you meet the rest of the bunch," Jamie told her. "As cute as Conor is, he's not my type. But Ryan has this cousin, Colm, that I would go for in a minute if I had to choose a man."

"Maybe I'd better not meet the rest. I'm already lusting in my heart over this one!"

After thoroughly tiring the baby out, Conor left at around nine, giving all of the assembled women hugs, reserving kisses for his sister, Caitlin and Jamie.

The baby was asleep in Ryan's arms, and they all said goodnight as soon as Conor drove away. "I don't remember getting that nap today, Ms. Evans," Ryan said to Jamie as they all ascended the stairs.

"Let me put her to bed," Catherine offered, reaching for the sleeping bundle as they reached the top of the stairs.

"Are you sure?" Ryan asked, handing Caitlin over quickly.

"I'd love to. Now you two get some rest. We're going to have a very busy day tomorrow."

After a quick round of quiet wishes for a good night's sleep, Catherine made for the nursery, with Jamie and Ryan heading to their room.

Jamie lingered in the bath for a while after Ryan finished. Coming out, she was slightly disappointed to hear the soft snores that characterized Ryan's deepest sleep. *Well, there goes our last chance for a little love until Thursday. No way we'll have any time alone in Disneyland.* She slid into bed, smiling to herself when Ryan immediately curled around her body, instinctively seeking her in sleep. *Ah well, having her close to me like this is worth more than all of the sex in the world*, she thought fondly, grasping Ryan's limp hand and placing it on her hip, just like her partner would have done if she had been awake.

Caitlin began to fuss just before five. She was merely wet, not hungry, and after Ryan changed her and sang her a song, she drifted back into a contented sleep, seemingly happy to remain in her crib. Ryan trudged into the bath to relieve herself, and while there, she brushed her teeth mechanically. After she washed her face a smile broke out across her handsome features, and she immediately went back into their room and crawled into bed. She snuggled up against Jamie's warm back and slowly began to stroke her thighs. After a few minutes she felt her begin to stir, and soon thereafter Jamie began to move against her. "Need some love, Tiger?" Jamie asked in a sleepy voice.

Ryan snuggled even closer and nodded her head against her lover's neck. Jamie rolled over and caught sight of the hopeful, desire filled, clear blue eyes. She couldn't resist the little grin that curled the edges of Ryan's sexy mouth, so she opened her arms and said, "Works for me."

Ryan's hair-trigger lust was easily and swiftly satisfied, and they were sound asleep again by 5:30. They snuggled into each other's arms and didn't stir until 7:30 when Jamie finally had to answer nature's call. When she came back Ryan was still in bed, stretching sensually.

"I wish I had time to nibble on you again, but I think we need to get going," Jamie said. Even though it was time to go, she couldn't resist jumping onto the bed for one last cuddle. "You've never woken me up in the middle of the night before. Is this a trend?"

"You didn't mind did you?" Ryan asked tentatively. "I probably should have just waited until you woke up, but I was…"

Jamie touched her lips with her fingers, then kissed her. "I didn't mind a bit. When you're in that mood I can practically blow on you and satisfy you. What time was it, anyway?"

"I think it was around five."

"It was totally hot to feel your warms hands running all over my body while I was waking. I think I was in a kind of erotic fog. It really felt great."

"I don't think this is a trend," Ryan mused, answering Jamie's earlier question. "I'm still a little needy from being away from you, and I guess I have to build up some love reserves."

"I enjoyed it, but I think once a night is my limit. If you need more than that you're gonna have to go with Lefty," she said as she grasped the hand in question and bestowed a kiss on each of the fingers.

During their joint shower, Ryan continued to rub against her partner in such a sensual manner that Jamie finally brought the hand held shower down and satisfied her once again. The sight of Ryan's sexy body backed up against the tile with her arms spread wide for support, and her hips gyrating, caused Jamie to heat up as well, so Ryan returned the favor moments later. Nuzzling close to her partner as her heart slowed, Ryan murmured, "Will that hold you for two days of abstinence?"

"Yes," Jamie purred, shifting her hips a few last times. "I'm good. I'm very good. Nice and clean, too," she chuckled, guessing that even her cervix had gotten a good rinse.

"Having sex in the shower is kinda nice," Ryan agreed. "Sex and cleanup all in one swoop."

"Yeah, that part is nice, but it's hard to keep standing when I come. That really takes some discipline."

"Piker," Ryan scoffed, not taking the time to regale Jamie with some of her most challenging orgasmic accomplishments.

Since the crib was empty, the women went in search of their charge, finding her enjoying breakfast, nestled happily in Catherine's arms. She was wearing a new outfit that Catherine had obviously just purchased for her. Tiny madras shorts in blue, yellow, green, and fuchsia topped off with a canary yellow T-shirt made her look summery and bright. Her babysitters were also wearing shorts, Ryan in navy blue and Jamie in khaki. Ryan wore her favorite navy blue and white vintage Hawaiian shirt, while

Jamie favored a spaghetti-strapped tank top in dark khaki green covered by a yellow cotton blouse that she had left half unbuttoned.

Catherine was wearing a pair of off-white cotton duck slacks that fit close to her slim body. A summery print blouse in yellow, pale blue, and off-white hung out over the slacks, with a pale yellow sweater tied over her shoulders in much the same style that Jamie often adopted.

When breakfast was finished they got the car packed, nearly filling the trunk of the Lexus. Ryan checked the car seat one last time before she brought the baby down, since they had moved it to Catherine's car the day before. Her attention was caught by a golden glimmer under the car seat. Reaching under the seatbelt, she extracted the chain and medallion that Catherine had been wearing on Sunday.

Pensively examining the primitive design, she handed it back to Catherine when she went back inside. "I found this in the car."

"I wondered where that had gone to," Catherine said. "Thank you, Ryan."

"What type of medallion is that?"

"Oh, it's an Etruscan coin," Catherine said, going back into the kitchen to get her things.

She lets the baby chew on a coin minted by people who inhabited Italy thousands of years ago. My Lord, this lifestyle is gonna take some getting used to!

As they pulled away from the house, Ryan instructed Caitlin to wave goodbye, and the baby dutifully complied.

"Boy, she's really got that bye-bye thing down, doesn't she?" Jamie asked.

"Yeah, it just got locked in last week. Annie said that she woke up one morning and just seemed to understand that the wave went together with people leaving, and she's been doing it ever since. Now she just needs the words to go with it."

"She does seem a little reluctant to speak real words," Jamie said as Caitlin babbled away in the back seat.

"Uhm, I wasn't gonna tell you this, but she said her first clear words on Sunday at Mass."

"You weren't gonna tell me? Why not?"

"I don't want the rest of the family to know," she explained. "It would kill Annie if she knew she'd missed it, and given the scenario, I was afraid of being the butt of another family joke."

"What? I don't get it."

"We were up at the altar during the Eucharistic Prayer. Sara was holding her when we started making the sign of peace. I was obviously a little too far away for Caitlin's pleasure so she decided to call me back."

"She said your name?" Jamie asked.

"No," she said slowly. "She called me Da-Da." She shrugged her shoulders and smirked.

Jamie threw her head back and laughed so hard tears came to her eyes, Catherine, laughing along, said, "Oh Ryan, that is too precious. Did she say it very loud?"

"I think the people in the last pew heard her," she admitted.

"Oh God, that must have been hilarious," Jamie said as she shook her head. "But I guess you could plead that she was just vocalizing, since she used the wrong name for you."

"She'd better not do it again. Tommy will have my hide if I get his name."

"It will be interesting to see what she calls you. Your name is going to be tough for her."

"Yeah, I guess it is. She can do 'm's and 'b's and 'd's, but that's about it right now. I think it will be a while before she can handle an 'r'."

"Well, I promise not to tell anyone she did it, but I'm going to put it in my journal and tell her about it when she's older. She'll get a kick out of it."

As they approached the airport, they tuned the radio to the information station and were pleased to learn that the long-term parking lot was still open. To avoid too much hassle Ryan dropped her passengers off at the terminal so all of Caitlin's gear could be checked. They had decided to bring her jogger even though they knew they would be able to rent a stroller at the park. Ryan's stated reason was that they wouldn't have strollers as nice as this one, but secretly she thought she might get up early and take the baby for a run around Anaheim. They also carried the car seat, which added a significant amount of bulk, but was necessary for the trip from the airport to the park. A small thermal chest carried nine frozen containers of breast milk, and Caitlin's backpack contained stuffed animals, toys, and soft books. Her tiny suitcase housed twenty diapers, twelve jars of baby food, and six complete outfits.

For her part, Ryan carried her favorite backpack, one that she had suffered a good bit of teasing over when she was in Santa Cruz. "I happen to like Bad Batz Muru," she had told Jordan. "He's the only 'Hello Kitty' character I liked as a child, and I still have the backpack." The small pack held another pair of shorts, two cotton shirts, two pairs of undershorts, her swimsuit, her toothbrush, and a bottle of sun block. She chose to travel very light since she had decided that Catherine and Jamie would surely bring anything else she could possibly need.

When Ryan arrived at the gate, Catherine was sitting in a chair playing cheerfully with an equally happy baby. She was holding an adorable pair of stuffed terrycloth toys, one representing Pluto and the other Goofy. She would put the toys behind her bag on the next seat and slowly raise them up so they peeked over the top. Every time they showed their heads she would cry, "Peek-a-boo," and Caitlin would squeal with delight.

Ryan came up from behind and bent over to kiss her cheek. "She's on the verge of really understanding this," she said. "It's so cute to watch her think this through." After studying the props, she added, "Those are very cute little toys. Did you buy them for her yesterday?"

"Yes, and I double checked with the clerk to make sure they were age appropriate. There are no buttons or anything else that can get loose, so she can put them in her mouth safely," she said rather proudly.

"You did a very good job," Ryan congratulated her. "New toys are always a good idea before a trip. Where did Jamie go?"

"She wanted to buy a couple of biscotti for the baby. After seeing how she reacted to the one on Sunday, I'd say it was a good choice."

"Indeed. Cait's loved them for months now. I just hope Jamie brings one for me too."

She spotted Jamie's blonde head coming down the hallway, craning her neck to make eye contact. Jamie's face broke into an adorable grin when she saw her, and Catherine had to smile also. As Jamie approached she held out a big biscotti and dangled it over the head of her lover, who eventually jumped up and snagged it with her teeth. "Being around you two is so refreshing," Catherine said. "I feel ten years younger when we're together."

"Really?" Ryan asked as she extracted her prize from her mouth. "Why's that?"

"Oh, most of my friends are relatively unhappy about some aspect of their lives. I love them all dearly but sometimes I need to be around happy people."

Jamie smiled at her mother, confiding, "If I were any happier I'd burst."

Caitlin looked up at the three of them and giggled wildly, showing them all the face of true joy.

"Ryan," Catherine said as she looked at the floor near her feet, "I didn't notice your suitcase when we checked our things. Where is it?"

"Right here," she said, holding up the half empty backpack. "I didn't think I'd need much."

Catherine gave her an indulgent grin, mentioning to her daughter, "I don't think I've ever said those words."

As they waited for the announcement to board, Ryan spent the time observing Catherine with the baby. She really did seem relaxed and youthful as she laughed and played with her happy young friend. *Everyone will assume that Catherine is Caitlin's mom. With that new haircut she looks exactly the right age to have a child.* Gazing from Jamie to Catherine to Caitlin, she decided, *Actually, I'm the only one who* doesn't *look like I'm related to Caitlin.*

They were called to board right on time. Ryan looked askance when Catherine went to the front of the line, but when she signaled to her companions they followed right behind. Catherine presented their tickets to the attendant and when they were immediately whisked aboard, Ryan fought to hold her tongue at the realization that Catherine had booked them into first class seats, including one for the baby

Okay, you told Catherine to make the arrangements. She made them. So shut up already. It's her money, she's got more than she knows what

to do with, and she's having a ball. Worse things could happen. The spacious first class cabin featured only four seats across—two on each side of the aisle. Catherine insisted that she wanted to sit with the baby, so they finally agreed that she would sit by the window with Caitlin on the aisle. Ryan would sit on the adjacent aisle seat with Jamie by her side.

Ryan felt good about having the car seat for the baby, but she knew that Caitlin didn't share her opinion. The baby wasn't wild about sitting in the seat even in the car, so she assumed that she would be even more antagonistic towards it on the plane. So to avoid strife for as long as possible they decided to wait until the last minute to strap her in.

A few minutes before their scheduled departure, the flight attendant came by to introduce himself. "Hi," he said to Catherine. "I'm Scott. If you need anything for your baby just let me know." He got down on his haunches and spoke to Caitlin for a few moments, much to her delight. "She's just precious," he said. "How old is she?"

Catherine just winged it as she confidently replied, "Eleven months. Her name is Caitlin."

"Well, Caitlin," he said, "I hope you have fun today."

"It's her first flight," Catherine said. "Do you have any tips?"

"It usually helps if you give her a bottle," he said. "Swallowing keeps their ears open. Most babies really hate takeoffs, so don't be surprised if she screams."

"Can you warm a bottle for me?" Catherine asked, having made sure there was one in the backpack that they carried on.

"Sure. Let me pop it in the microwave right now."

"Oh, no," Catherine said immediately, having learned her lesson from Ryan. "It's breast milk. Could you heat it by running warm water over it?"

"Sure. No problem," he agreed. "We should be taxiing to the runway in a few minutes, but we'll probably have a wait for clearance. Even though the seat belt light will go on, don't bother putting her in her car seat right then. I'll come tell you when we've been cleared."

"Thank you, Scott," she said, giving him a winning smile.

"No problem. Babies are my favorite passengers," he said, patting the baby lightly on the head. Catherine took out a bottle from the backpack under her seat and handed it to Scott. As he walked away, the seat belt light came on and the pilot announced that they were ready to depart.

Scott scampered back with the warmed formula and announced that they had been cleared immediately. "We're next," he said. "Buckle her up!"

Ryan leapt across the aisle to secure Caitlin into her seat. She worked very quickly and managed to get the baby settled and hop back into her own seat just as they started to taxi. Catherine placed the bottle into Caitlin's mouth and she started to suck away. She'd been up since six and it was getting close to naptime, but they all expected that the excitement of the day would disrupt her schedule. To everyone's amazement, she settled down into her seat and leaned her head back as her eyes started to blink much more slowly. The cabin was rattling and shaking as the sound of the engines filled the plane, but the noisier it got, the more relaxed Caitlin became. She gave a small start when the wheels tucked into their housings, but other than that she was completely oblivious to the entire procedure.

Ryan looked up from Caitlin's sleeping form to notice both Catherine and Jamie staring at the baby in open-mouthed astonishment. She caught Catherine's eye and gave her a little shrug along with a bemused grin. Catherine shook her head as a gentle smile covered her face. She placed her hand on the baby's head and tenderly stroked her sleeping face as she gazed at her. She finally tore her eyes away and said, "That's just how Jamie was. The first flight we took was to Europe when she was about five months old. She slept through the takeoff like she was born to fly," she fondly recollected.

"I didn't know that," Jamie said as she leaned over Ryan to make eye contact with her mother.

"I was totally surprised at how you behaved. I thought you'd hate it because I'd heard all of these horror stories about babies screaming for twelve hours straight. But you never seemed to mind flying. You know, part of the reason I'm so enthralled with this little one is that she reminds me so much of you. You were sweet and happy and calm, just like she is."

"Oh, she's far from calm when Ryan gets her riled up," Jamie assured her mother. "But she is awfully happy." She looked down at the baby for a few moments, then asked, "Was I really happy like that?"

"Oh yes," she assured her daughter. "I always got two compliments about you. One was how beautiful you were, and the other was how happy you were. You weren't very loud, and you didn't like to go to strangers like Caitlin does, but you were definitely happy." She gave Jamie a concerned look and asked, "Does that surprise you?"

"No, I suppose not. It's just that you've rarely talked about how I was as a baby. I guess I assumed that you didn't have anything positive to say."

"Well, we're going to remedy that, Jamie. I have nothing but positive things to say about your youth, and you're going to hear little tidbits every time I think of one."

Jamie graced her with a beaming smile as she admitted, "I'd really like that, Mom."

She settled back into her chair and Ryan brought her lips close to her ear to ask, "When did you start calling her Mom? I noticed it yesterday, but I forgot to ask."

"In Rhode Island. She just started to seem like a mom."

"I'm glad," Ryan said, threading her fingers through Jamie's. "Mother always sounded more like an obligatory title than a term of affection."

"I think it was," Jamie admitted as she leaned her chair back to take her own morning nap. Within minutes her head had dropped to the side, and Ryan lifted the armrest and scooted closer so her partner could avail herself of her shoulder. Jamie slept peacefully for nearly an hour, finally waking to find Ryan's head resting on her own. Even in the awkward position she was fairly comfortable nestled into the warm body, so she closed her eyes again and rested until the pilot announced that they were approaching L.A.

Ryan's head popped up as soon as the pilot made the announcement. Jamie once again marveled at her ability to wake so quickly, noting that her eyes were bright and focused and a happy smile graced her face. "Sleep well, honey?"

"Yeah," Ryan purred, launching into a shortened version of her stretching routine, as befitted her quick nap. Jamie rubbed her back briskly as Ryan leaned over to unkink while Catherine watched their routine with an amused grin. Jamie looked over at her mother with a little shrug as she explained, "She gets stiff when she sleeps. Even in a first class seat, that's a lot of body to fold into a small space."

"You should see me flying coach to Ireland," Ryan smirked. "I pop in and out of my seat so many times that I look like a jumping jack."

"Your coach days are over," Jamie declared, giving Ryan one of her best "don't argue with me" looks.

"That's where you're wrong, punkin," Ryan averred, tweaking Jamie's nose playfully. "My teams fly coach. I've got a full year of tiny seats on tiny planes to look forward to."

"Tiny planes?" Catherine asked.

"Yeah. We have to go to Corvallis, Oregon and Pullman, Washington, and large commercial jets don't fly there."

"You could always charter a private jet..." Catherine began, but Ryan dropped her chin and narrowed her eyes, giving her mother-in-law a stern look of warning.

"Oh, my," the older woman said. "Is that the look of someone who's putting her foot down?"

"It is," Jamie decided, leaning over Ryan to double check. "The eyes get very narrow, see," she indicated, drawing her index finger down the ridge of furrowed skin between Ryan's eyes. "And the mouth becomes a grim line." She tried to insert a finger between Ryan's lips, but they were pressed together so forcefully that she couldn't make any headway. Unable to maintain her scowl while she was being played with, Ryan burst into a fit of giggles, her eyes dancing merrily as Jamie gave her a good tickle.

Catherine gazed at the playful pair. "I find it amusing how comfortable you seem with each other. You act like you've been together for years, rather than weeks."

"I've got to admit that it feels that way to me," Jamie admitted, slipping an arm around her partner. "But even though we've only been intimate for a little while, we spent a ton of time together before that. We just know each other really well," she added as she continued to rub Ryan's back, to her obvious pleasure.

The seat belt light came on and Scott, the flight attendant, came by to check on everyone. Caitlin looked like she was about to wake up since her little hands had begun to twitch, but she stayed asleep until the plane actually hit the runway. When the cabin bounced heavily, her head jerked up and her eyes flew open.

While the plane continued to bounce, the engines roared mightily as they worked to slow the craft. Her little face began to scrunch up into a frown and Ryan prepared herself for a scream, but the baby turned her head and caught sight of Ryan and Jamie and after a few blinks, a sweet smile settled onto her face. The adults all smiled back, and within seconds she was gurgling and wriggling around in her seat. Even though they were still rolling towards the gate Ryan thought it safe to remove her, so Catherine began the extraction.

Once free, Caitlin settled happily onto Catherine's lap, accepting her après-nap snuggles from this relative stranger. Her T-shirt was damp with sweat but Ryan decided to leave it on her, given the 80-degree temperature that the pilot had just announced.

"Toss her over and I'll go change her before we get off," Ryan suggested.

"I'll do it," Catherine replied confidently as she pulled a fresh diaper and a packet of baby wipes from the backpack. She settled the baby onto her hip and made her way to the restroom, leaving both Ryan and Jamie to stare after her in shock.

"She wants to change her diaper?" Jamie asked slowly. "I don't know that she's ever done that before."

"Are you sure they didn't switch mothers on you when you were in Rhode Island? She sure seems like a different person."

"I don't know what happened, but I'm not complaining," Jamie decided.

Twenty minutes later they were cruising out of LAX in a full-sized limousine. Ryan was busy playing with all of the buttons and gadgets, much to the amusement of Catherine and Jamie. "Hey look," she said, too loudly for the small space, "there's a refrigerator!" She continued to scoot around on the big seat facing her companions, trying to take in all of the amenities.

"Haven't you ever been in a limo before?" Catherine asked, charmed by the young woman's boundless enthusiasm.

"Uhm, just for my mother's funeral," she replied rather absently as she found the remote control for the TV. "Check it out. We can watch a movie."

Catherine didn't know if she should apologize for her question, but since Ryan seemed so happy she assumed that she hadn't put a damper on her mood. "Not even for your prom?" the older woman asked, to steer the conversation onto a brighter note.

"Nope. Never had a date with a boy, and none of the girls would go with me." She waggled her right eyebrow, fixing Catherine with a devilish grin. "Believe me, I asked."

Catherine looked completely flabbergasted at this revelation. "You've never been with a man?"

"Neither man nor boy," she confirmed.

"She's untouched by the Y chromosome," Jamie said with a chuckle. "Although not many double X's have escaped her."

Catherine tried to hide her amazement, but she had a tough time of it. "I just assumed that most women would experiment with men and then decide it wasn't right for them. I mean...I don't want to be indelicate, but how can you be sure you're gay if you've never even been kissed by a man?"

Ryan gave her a deceptively innocent smile as she asked, "How many women have you kissed?"

Jamie was afraid she was going to have to catch her mother's eyeballs as they popped out of her head, but Catherine quickly regained her composure. "Well, none."

"Then how do you know you're not a lesbian?" Ryan followed up with the logical corollary.

Catherine just shook her head as she turned to Jamie and said, "She's a quick one, isn't she?"

"Extremely," Jamie agreed, blowing Ryan a kiss.

The rest of the ride was spent retrieving Caitlin's plastic blocks as she sat in her car seat and threw them. Her desire to play the game was unquenchable, and by the time they reached Anaheim, Catherine was marveling at Ryan's patience. "Ryan, you've been picking up those same toys for over an hour. She's certainly got you well trained."

Ryan gave her a puzzled look as she replied, "Trained? She's not training me, she's thinking."

"Thinking? It looks to me like she's training you to satisfy her needs."

"Well, that's true, after a fashion. But I think her need right now is to test a theory."

"Whatever do you mean?"

"The only way she learns anything is by doing experiments. Like any good scientist, she has to do them often enough, and under varied conditions, to make sure the results aren't just a fluke."

"What is she testing now?" Catherine asked, her dark eyes holding a hint of challenge.

"I think she's trying to prove that the block gets to the floor because of her actions. She's just at the very beginning of understanding cause and effect. It looks to me like she's just discovered that she is the cause of the block hitting the floor. I honestly don't think the effect is all that important to her yet."

"Don't try to argue with her about scientific theories, Mom. She'll make your head throb," Jamie said.

"I'm sure of that," she agreed gamely as Ryan bent to pick up the block one more time. She was obviously unable to concede the point, however, because she pointed out, "Why does she look at you after she throws it, if she's not trying to make you retrieve it?"

"She does watch me, but watch *how* she watches me." All three women kept a close watch on exactly where Caitlin focused during the next round.

"It looks like she's watching your face," Jamie observed.

"Precisely. I think she's watching to see if I share her joy about this new discovery. If she was just trying to make me do something, I think she would watch the toy—but she seems to lose interest in the toy as soon as she releases it. See," she said, handing the block back again, "as soon as she tosses it, she looks at me. When I smile back at her to encourage her, she gets excited. I really think we're sharing a moment."

Catherine shook her head, then turned to Jamie. "Does she put this much thought into everything?"

"Yep," she conceded as she shot her lover an affectionate glance. "I don't think she does anything that she hasn't considered thoroughly."

"I think Da might disagree with you," Ryan gently reminded her. "I think his most common question when I was growing up was, 'Siobhán, do you *ever* think before you act?'"

Ryan hadn't bothered to ask where they were staying, and she was a bit surprised when they headed into the Disneyland Hotel. She had secretly thought they'd be staying in some elegant little hotel and taking a cab to the park, and was pleased to find that they were going to be right in the midst of things.

As a bellman unloaded their bags, Ryan removed the car seat with Caitlin still in it. It wasn't the easiest thing to carry the baby in the seat, but she thought it made more sense than carrying both separately, especially given how crowded the lobby was. When they got inside, Catherine assessed the situation quickly, spotting a sign that said "Concierge Check-In". "Be right back," she said, setting off confidently.

Cait wanted out of her restraints to join the dozens of kids lounging on the floor in front of a large screen television watching "The Mighty Ducks," but Ryan knew that was a loser bet, so she tried to distract her while they waited. Thankfully, Catherine handled things quickly, and she was back in a few moments, bearing plastic key cards for each of them.

Their rooms were on the top floor of the Sierra building, and Ryan was impressed to find that Catherine had reserved a suite. The two bedrooms flanking the common living room were both generously sized, and one held a roll-away crib. "You've done well here, Catherine," Ryan complimented her as she went to the room with the crib.

"Why don't you let me sleep with the baby?" Catherine asked, stopping Ryan in her tracks.

"That's beyond generous of you to offer, but she's often a little frightened when she wakes in the middle of the night. I think it would freak her out if I wasn't there."

"I just thought you girls could use some alone time," she persisted.

"We're fine, Catherine," Ryan insisted. "Really." Jamie was quiet during this interchange, knowing that Ryan understood Caitlin's needs better than she. She really didn't mind having the baby in their room—had, in fact, expected it—but she was touched that her mother was so generously offering to watch her through the night.

"All right, dear, I'm sure you know best. I just hope that you'll take some time to be alone if you need it."

"We will," Jamie piped up. "Thanks, Mom."

After a quick reassurance call to Annie and Tommy, Ryan spent a good deal of time carrying Caitlin around to investigate every nook and cranny of their rooms. When she came back into the large communal living area she nearly shrieked with delight when she spied the large basket filled with fruit, wine, cheese, and chocolate. "Jamie, look! They left us food!"

Jamie gave her a high wattage grin as she came over to offer a hug. "Good food, too, from the looks of it." Turning to her mother, she asked, "How did you manage to get this great room in the middle of the summer with one day's notice?"

"Oh, I have some contacts in the Disney organization," she said lightly as she carried her bag into the smaller of the two bedrooms.

"Mother…," Jamie called after her, "spill it."

"Okay," she agreed as she came back into the main room. "I worked to help secure funding for the new symphony hall being built in LA. I made some friends through my work who were able to help me pull a few strings."

"Is that your complete statement?" Jamie asked, imitating her father's questioning style.

"Yes, dear, that's my story and I'm sticking to it. Now let's get some lunch."

"Isn't this lunch?" Ryan asked as she busily sorted all of the foodstuffs located in the big basket. "We've got enough wine to get us well oiled, plus soakage!"

Seeing Catherine's puzzled look, Jamie said, "She throws in an Irish expression every once in a while just to keep you on your toes. I think that one means we've got food and drink."

"Mighty!" Ryan agreed enthusiastically.

"It's hard enough to keep up with her when she's speaking English," Catherine moaned.

Chapter Three

They decided to go to the PCH Grill for lunch, and Ryan brought all of the brochures and documents that Catherine had been given at check-in. She pored over the material as though she were drawing up a campaign to invade a foreign country, finally coming up with a master plan that she was happy with.

Ryan folded her hands on the table, looking at each of her adult companions, an expectant look on her handsome face. "Well?" Jamie asked, knowing that her partner wanted to share, but that she liked to be cajoled a bit.

"Well, what?" The dark head cocked slightly, bright blue eyes shimmering with impish pleasure.

"Spill it, General Schwartzkopf. I know you have every minute planned."

"Not every minute," Ryan scoffed. "I've allowed for one hour a day for personal time. You may spend that as you wish."

"Buffy…" Jamie threatened, narrowing her gaze.

"Okay," Ryan said, grinning with excitement. "Here's the plan. We wait until little bits is ready for her nap. Then we go on the 'Welcome to Disneyland Tour' that's part of the package. I don't think the baby would like it, and it's only an hour and a half, so we could go and be back while she sleeps. This presupposes that you don't mind watching her," Ryan said, addressing Catherine.

"Of course not," Catherine agreed. "I could use a nap as well."

"Okay, we're set," Ryan declared, smiling at the server as lunch was delivered.

"That's it?" Jamie asked. "That's all you've planned?"

"Nope. The rest is on a need-to-know basis," she said, giving her partner a fiendish grin.

Caitlin was pretty riled up after lunch, and Ryan decided that she needed some cuddling and calming to get ready to nap. So she took the baby into their room and sat on a comfortable chair to read to her from one of her storybooks.

The Evans women sat in the living room and chatted while Ryan performed her "sand man" act.

They had been chatting for just a few minutes when Catherine's cell phone rang. Finding the device, she hit the button and said, "Hello."

Jamie's brow furrowed when her mother's face fell, a pained look crossing her features for just a moment before a familiar mask of studied indifference settled there. "I didn't have plans to do this before, Jim," she said as she got up to go to her room. "You don't need to speak to me in that tone," she snapped as the door closed, preventing Jamie from hearing the rest.

She was gone only a few minutes, her composure back in place when she re-entered the living room. "I'm sorry about that, honey. I don't like for you to hear that type of bickering."

Jamie looked up, focusing her eyes on her mother's face as Catherine sat back down. "Mom, will you level with me?"

Catherine blinked a few times, finally nodding her head slowly. "Of course, dear. What do you want to know?"

"Is my relationship with Ryan putting stress on your marriage? I...I couldn't stand it if I thought you were having trouble because of me."

"Come here, Jamie," Catherine said softly, patting the cushion next to her. The younger woman crossed the room and sat next to her mother, automatically leaning on her shoulder. "Yes, your father and I are having problems. But, no, it's not because of you."

"It seems like more than a coincidence, Mom. I mean, I've never heard you argue about things…"

"Jamie, just because we don't argue doesn't mean that everything is all right. A little arguing is a good sign. It shows that you care enough to feel hurt."

"Are you hurt, Mom?" she asked with concern, reaching over to grasp her mother's hand.

"Yes, dear, I'm hurt, and I'm sure that your father is, too. He wouldn't behave as he has been if he wasn't acting out of fear and pain."

Jamie's brow furrowed. She thought that her father had no reason to feel anything other than shame for the way he treated Ryan. "Why is he hurt?"

"I doubt that you look at it this way, but he's had to deal with some very big changes in the last six months, and he hasn't handled them well. I think it really shook him when you broke up with Jack, even though I doubt that he ever told you that."

"No, he didn't," she said, shaking her head in confusion. "But why…?"

"I think he liked the path you were on. It mirrored the choices he would have made for you. I think he felt that he'd done his job as a parent, and now you would go on your way and give credence to his choices by making the same ones for yourself."

Jamie nodded, realizing for the first time that her breaking up with Jack might have seemed like a slap in the face to her father.

"Your falling in love with Ryan put a fine point on your decision to follow your own path. This isn't what he wants for you, and it isn't who he thinks you are. It's made him question your entire relationship, honey. So, as angry as I've been with him, I still have some empathy for how this has hurt him, and I hope that you can find some of that in your heart, too."

"It will take a while, Mom," she said, honestly. "He's going to have to back off from harassing Ryan, or I'll never forgive him."

Catherine nodded, knowing that her child had just as hard a time forgiving people as her husband did.

"So why is he angry with you, Mom? You didn't encourage my choices."

"Of course I did," Catherine corrected. "Not at first, of course, but as time goes on, and I've realized how right this is for you, I've been very supportive. I would honestly say that this is the first time in our relationship that I have openly defied him, and it's not easy for him to take. It's making him lash out."

"So it *is* my fault," Jamie moaned. "I knew that he was angry with me and taking it out on you."

"That's not truc," Catherine assured her. "It's about time we had a disagreement. We've been like business partners for years now, but I was the silent partner, letting him make all of the decisions. I think this will either make us examine our marriage and try to fix it or…" she trailed off, not wanting to say the words.

Jamie released her hold and slumped back onto the sofa. "I just didn't have any idea. I thought you were happy."

"We weren't unhappy," she assured her. "We've each played our part, and kept up the façade, but we haven't had any emotional spark in a long, long while."

"How long?" Jamie asked tentatively, not having any idea when things had changed for her parents.

Catherine looked like she was not going to answer but she finally said, "I'd say at least 15 years."

"15 years!" Jamie cried. "You've only been married 22. What in the world happened?"

Catherine patted her thigh in a comforting manner, saying, "Maybe some day we can talk about this. But I don't think this is the time."

Jamie looked over at her with her face full of unanswered questions. "But hearing this makes me worry, Mom. Now I feel that I need to be the peacemaker so that you and Daddy don't divorce." Her stomach was pulsing in a knot of tension, and she knew that she was moments from being sick.

Catherine saw the warning signs on her daughter's pale face with the slightly green cast beneath her pallor. She knew that she needed to reassure her, but she didn't want to lie to her, so she was torn about what to say.

Not getting her answers fast enough, Jamie tried again. "You say that you've had trouble for over 15 years. Do you think you got married too young? Is that part of the problem?"

"I'm certain of it," Catherine said in an unguarded moment, the truth of the question hitting her hard. "It was too soon, and too rapid, especially for your father."

"Then why did you do it so soon? It's not like you had to..."

Catherine didn't respond directly. She just gazed at her daughter's pain-filled features and felt like her heart would break at the anguish she saw reflected in the watery green eyes. Jamie held her gaze until the answer became obvious to her. "You...had to."

An almost imperceptible nod was her answer. Catherine looked down at the floor with a look of shame. "I think he's always blamed me for that."

Jamie was too stunned to move at this point. She heard Ryan open the door from their room, but it closed again just a few seconds later. Catherine scooted closer and slid her arms around her daughter as she whispered, "You were the best mistake I've ever made. Both of us were overjoyed to have you. It was just a little earlier than we had planned."

Jamie took a deep breath and asked the question that was burning in her mind. "Did you ever consider…aborting me?"

Catherine sat up in alarm as she cried, "No! Not for a second. We never even discussed that, Jamie."

There was something in her mother's statement that niggled in the back of her mind, and she asked, "Who did discuss it? Did someone try to talk you into having an abortion?"

Catherine mentally cursed her daughter's perceptiveness, wishing that she could lie and answer in the negative. But she knew that her face would betray her lie, and she didn't want to perpetuate any more lies or half truths. She nodded slowly, her head moving almost imperceptibly.

"Who?" Jamie asked, her voice quiet, yet determined.

"My mother," Catherine finally whispered. "She felt that I was ruining my life getting married so young. She…she didn't think of you as a person, Jamie, please believe that."

The younger woman nodded, understanding that an unplanned pregnancy could seem like nothing more than an inconvenience depending on your perspective. "You thought of me as a person, didn't you?' she asked, somehow knowing the answer.

"From the first day," Catherine whispered, wrapping her in a bruising embrace. "As much tumult as it caused, I knew from the first day that you were going to be a gift to us, Jamie. I've never—not for one minute—regretted my decision to give birth to you." She sniffed a few times, her composure shot, as she added, "Neither has your father. He wasn't really ready to get married, but he was never unhappy about you. It was just the timing that was hard for him."

Jamie closed her eyes and nodded as she took in a deep breath. "I believe you, Mom. It's just a shock for me. One of the things I always believed was that you were both very much in love, and that your decision to have me was just that…a decision. It's hard to hear that my arrival caused you to decide to marry."

"You caused us to decide to marry sooner than we might have," Catherine corrected, "but I believe we would have done so anyway, Jamie, I really do. I loved your father and I really wanted to build a life with him. I can't speak for him, but I believe he loved me too."

"Do you still love him?"

"Yes, I do," she replied without hesitation. "But I don't like him much at the moment."

"I don't like him much either," Jamie agreed, "but I don't think I could ever stop loving him."

"He doesn't make it easy sometimes. He can be a difficult man to love."

They were quiet for a few moments, their arms still wrapped around each other, when Ryan's dark head poked through the door again.

"Come on in, honey," Jamie said, sitting up and extending a hand in Ryan's direction. When Ryan settled her frame onto the couch, Jamie leaned into her, placing her head on Ryan's chest to allow for a much needed hug. The silence was uncomfortable, but Ryan wasn't about to ask why both women had been crying. She just offered as much comfort as her body could convey, knowing that Jamie would tell her what was wrong when they were alone. "We'd better get going if we're going to make it back before Caitlin wakes," Jamie said as she regretfully pulled out of her grasp.

"I'm ready," Ryan said. "Are you sure you don't mind this, Catherine?"

"I not only don't mind, it's what I choose," she assured her.

As they headed for the door, Jamie reminded her, "I've got my phone on and I left the number right on the table. Call us if you need anything. Promise?"

"I promise," she said, sparing a fond smile for her daughter. "Now, go have fun."

As they hopped onto the monorail for the short ride to the park, Ryan tried to contain her enthusiasm over the transportation in order to gently ask, "Wanna talk about it?"

A small nod preceded Jamie's answer. "My parents had to get married, and now they might get divorced."

"What? Did your mom say that in so many words?"

"Which part?"

"About getting divorced," Ryan replied, eyes wide with alarm.

"Yes, basically she said that in so many words." After a beat she asked, "You're not surprised that she was pregnant?"

Ryan shrugged, conceding, "Not really. I thought as much when you told me how young she was when they got married. I also saw those pictures of their wedding, and it looked like it was the middle of the summer. That didn't add up to having you in February."

Jamie slapped herself in the forehead, muttering, "I've never known them to celebrate their anniversary. I have no idea when they got married."

"I'm not surprised your mom was pregnant, but I'm shocked that they might get divorced. She just seemed so accepting of your dad's behavior—like she was used to it."

"I think she is used to it, Ryan, but I also think she's had enough. I think she's finally trying to be an equal partner, and he doesn't like it."

Ryan looked at her as she bit her lip anxiously. "Jamie, I care very much about how all of this affects you, but there's a great big flower bed in the shape of Mickey's head, and I can see Sleeping Beauty's Castle, and it's getting to be too much for me to stay focused." The look on her face was nearly pleading, asking for permission to lose herself in the fantasy.

Willfully banishing the thoughts that zoomed through her head, Jamie took Ryan's hand and squeezed it. "We're here to have fun. Let's concentrate on that for a while. We can analyze this other stuff to death later."

Against all odds, the pair spent a totally enjoyable hour and a half on their tour. Summoning powers of denial that she didn't know she had, Jamie was able to lose herself in the moment, likely aided by Ryan's boundless enthusiasm for the entire experience. Ryan hopped around the tram like a three-year-old, bubbling with excitement as they were shown nearly every part of the park along with a good bit of the behind the scenes workings of the enterprise.

As soon as the tour was finished they rushed back to the room, the monorail expediting their journey. Ryan regaled Catherine with minute details of nearly everything they had seen, while Jamie went in to check on the baby. When she emerged from the bedroom 15 minutes later, she carried a gurgling infant with her. The baby wore a fresh diaper and nothing else as she held out her little arms to her cousin. Ryan gladly accepted the bundle and spent a few minutes talking softly to her, filling her in on the tour and their plans for the evening.

Jamie brought Catherine up to date simultaneously. "We thought we could go over to the park and have dinner and just walk around. They have a big parade at six that I think Caitlin would enjoy, so we'd like to do that. Then we thought we'd bring her back here and put her to bed. If we did that, would you be averse to watching her while we went back to go on some rides?"

"Not at all," Catherine said. "There are a couple of movies on pay-per-view that I'd like to see, and I'm in the middle of a fantastic book. I can easily entertain myself."

"Great. Let's go over around five so we can be sure to find a space to see the parade. You don't mind just grabbing a hot dog for dinner, do you?"

Catherine gave her daughter a fond smile as she teased, "You know how I love hot dogs. I have them almost constantly." At Jamie's droll grin, Catherine suggested, "Let me take care of dinner. I have an alternative to hot dogs that I think you'll be happy with."

"Okay," Jamie agreed as she joined her companions on the floor. Ryan was lying flat on her back and Caitlin was climbing all over her like she was a living jungle gym. Both the gymnast and the human apparatus were giggling as they played their little game. Before long Jamie had joined the game as an auxiliary gym, lying shoulder to shoulder with her partner as Caitlin expanded her territory. She poked and prodded and teased her big babysitters as she explored their faces with a thoroughness that amazed Catherine. Whatever part Caitlin grabbed, they would identify for her verbally and then touch her corresponding part in a more gentle fashion. Her concentration and enthusiasm seemed endless as they continued for nearly an hour, accompanied by Caitlin's frenzied laughter.

As they rode back to the park on the monorail, Catherine said, "You're so patient and calm with Caitlin, Ryan. Is that how you were raised?"

"I think so," she agreed reflectively. "I think my Aunt Maeve was the truly gifted one. She taught my parents a lot about raising children, according to my father."

"She's your father's sister?"

"No, she's my mother's older sister. According to my father, Maeve spent a terrific amount of time sharing her gifts when they had my brother Brendan. Her youngest was three or four when Brendan was born, so she had the opportunity to help out a lot."

"How did she learn?" Catherine asked.

"My father says it surely was not from my grandmother, and I'm inclined to agree," she said with a laugh. "I've spent a lot of time with my grandmother, and I must admit that her childrearing techniques are mostly along the lines of 'children should be seen and not heard'."

"That amazes me," Jamie said. "You've told me that she was strong willed, but I guess I assumed that she was the force behind all of the love in your family."

"No, that's doubtful. I think my grandfather was the one who made the girls feel loved and enabled them to express it so well."

"I wouldn't have guessed that," Jamie said thoughtfully. "I picture your grandmother as an older version of Maeve…all cute and sweet and loving."

"Lord no! And if you told them both that, I'm not sure who'd be more insulted."

"Are you serious?" Jamie asked. "I've never heard Maeve say a bad word about anyone."

"Oh, she'd never say a bad word about my grandmother, but it's pretty obvious they have their struggles. It doesn't take too much intuition to guess why a young woman would leave her home mere moments after she graduated from secondary school. She had no obvious skills, only enough money for the plane fare, and had never been farther from home than Dublin. So she had to be as interested in the leaving as she was in the adventure."

"Did she come alone?" Catherine asked, amazed that a young woman would be so bold.

"No, she came with a friend from school. My mother stayed in Ireland until she was 18, then she followed her, as every one knew she would, even though she was fairly happy in Ireland." Ryan smiled at Catherine and said, "You'll really like my aunt. She's quiet and very loving, but she has an inner strength that I envy. She had the misfortune of choosing the wrong man to marry, and she was in a loveless marriage most of her life, but none of her personal troubles ever seemed to dim her spirits. She's the epitome of a survivor, Catherine. She just has a pure heart that can't be dimmed, and I must say we're all lucky to have her."

"Is she still married?" Catherine asked.

"No, her husband died a little less than two years ago. They'd been separated for many years but they never divorced." A smile lit up Ryan's face. "She *is* going to marry again though."

"Really? That's lovely. You must be very happy for her."

"Oh, I am, but the rest of the family doesn't know yet. She's a bit afraid of the reaction she'll get when she informs everyone of her selection."

"Why would that be?"

"Because it's my father," she said, an impish grin covering her face.

Catherine looked puzzled for an instant but the light quickly dawned. "Oh. Marrying your deceased sister's husband might be a little too…"

"Yes. People might not like that," she conceded. "Plus, it'll be odd to get used to the two of them being in love. Da has been single since we were small, and Aunt Maeve has been alone for so long that you just don't expect that to change. But we all love her like a second mother, so I hope it'll go well."

"Will they live in your house?" Catherine asked, not having any idea of the size of the O'Flaherty manse.

"That's a big issue. My cousin Kevin lives with Maeve, and Rory and Conor live with Da. Plus, Jamie and I live there on the weekends. Our house is pretty big," she said, nearly causing Jamie's eyes to bug out of her head, "but it's full at this point. Maeve's house is quite small, so it's going to be hard to come up with a solution."

The monorail had reached its destination, and they spent the next few minutes getting through the crowds to reach Main Street and stake out a place in line. Catherine and Ryan sat on the curb to save spaces while Jamie carried Caitlin around in her baby sling to keep her occupied.

Catherine had obviously been thinking over the living situation for the O'Flaherty family because she asked, "Could your father buy a new house?"

"He'd have to use the proceeds from the sale of the old one, and he swears that he'll never throw any of us out. What we need is at least one big house to use as a gathering place for family events. Jamie mentioned that I have 14 male cousins in America, but only Tommy is married. We hardly fit in our house now. When they all start having kids it'll be mayhem."

Catherine had a hard time imagining what a house full of boisterous young men would be like, but then she remembered her days at Stanford and tried to recall how the fraternity houses had been, drawing an apt comparison. "What do you two want to do when you graduate? Do you want to stay in the East Bay?"

"No, I don't," Ryan said quickly, her face showing her discomfort with the idea. "I can't imagine living away from my family permanently. I really love Noe Valley and I want to make it our permanent home. I guess buying a house is something for the distant future, now that it looks like Jamie won't be able to control her money for quite a while."

"Ahh, now don't even think like that, Ryan. My husband has more than his share of faults, but he's not intentionally cruel. Just give him some time."

"We've got that, Catherine. I'd be happy to live in my room until we decide to start our family."

Catherine looked askance and asked, "Will that be a while?"

"Oh, I think so. I know how much work kids are. I want to enjoy being with Jamie for a good long while before we add to our responsibilities."

"That's good to hear," Catherine said, beaming a smile at her. "Don't make the same mistake I did in having a child before you're *both* fully ready."

Well, well, I guess she doesn't mind if I know the family secrets, Ryan mused. *Actually, she's really treating me like a member of the family.* Her pleasure was short lived as she considered, *now I only have to win Jim over.*

Much to everyone's pleasure, Caitlin turned out to be a big fan of parades. She sat on Ryan's shoulders and babbled away as she kicked her little legs so frequently and enthusiastically that Ryan was sure she would be a mass of bruises. But she gladly suffered for her little cousin, happy that the baby was enjoying herself so thoroughly. In truth, it was a toss-up as to who was having a better time. Ryan repeatedly turned to Jamie to point out some little tidbit that caught her watchful eye, and Jamie also enjoyed the extravaganza. Catherine was a bit overwhelmed to be surrounded by so many people and noise, but she handled it well.

She was having so much fun watching her daughter that she eventually ignored all of the noise and just focused on her.

For the thousandth time, she felt the sting of regret for having missed out on all of the chances to do things like this for Jamie when she was young. Once again she thanked the heavens for providing a second opportunity, even one coming this late in her daughter's youth.

When the parade was finished, they strolled along Main Street for a few minutes as Catherine started to get into the experience a little more. Shopping always got her involved, and she would have stayed in the stores a lot longer if Ryan hadn't finally put her foot down. By the time they started for dinner, Caitlin had a new navy blue swimsuit with little Mickey heads across the chest, a cute little yellow canvas hat to keep the sun from her eyes, 101 Dalmatians pajamas, a white T-shirt with Goofy embroidered on the pocket, and a matching pair of shorts in a blue and white check. But her most adorable gift was a pair of pink mouse ears with her name embroidered on the back. Unbeknownst to her partner, Jamie had purchased a matching pair for Ryan, and she snapped an adorable picture of both cousins with their ears on—Caitlin sitting happily on Ryan's shoulders. Ryan stared right into the camera with her relaxed, confident smile, and Jamie thought once again that Ryan could have easily made a very good living as a model. She was so completely comfortable with the camera, looking past the device to gaze into the photographer's eyes, and Jamie knew that was not a skill that was easy to teach.

Catherine expertly led them over to Adventureland with Jamie and Ryan pacing along behind. More than once Jamie informed her that there weren't any restaurants listed for that part of the park, but Catherine blithely ignored her warnings with the reply, "Trust me, dear."

When they reached the Pirates of the Caribbean she looked around carefully until she spotted a small gift shop called Pieces of Eight. Right next to the shop, an etched glass door bore the legend, 'Club 33'. Catherine rang the nearly hidden bell, and moments later a tuxedoed gentleman opened the door.

"Good evening," he said with a smile. "Have you dinner reservations?"

"Yes, we do," she answered. "Catherine Evans."

He scanned his list and quickly found her name. "Very good, Mrs. Evans," he responded. "Come right this way." Jamie and Ryan shared puzzled glances as the man led them up a staircase to a very elegant dining room on the second floor. The room was small, but each of the tables was generously sized. He pulled out chairs for each of them and quickly signaled someone to bring a seat for Caitlin. A large booster chair was brought out and properly secured to the wooden backed chair. Caitlin liked the freedom of the padded chair and didn't seem to mind having to be strapped in. As the menus were presented she began to babble quite loudly, but Jamie quickly stilled her with one of the biscotti that she still carried in her bag.

"Mother…" Jamie asked, drawing out the word, "how did we wind up here?"

"I told you I have some contacts." Catherine continued to scan the menu, her mouth curled up in a small smile.

"What is this place? And who did you have to call to get us in?"

"This is a private club for members and guests of the Disney organization, dear." Catherine sighed, put her menu down, and came clean. "I don't know if you're aware of it, but the new symphony hall is to be named for Walt Disney. His widow Lillian was one of the driving forces behind the idea. Well, Lillian died two years ago, and the hall has been mired in political and financial trouble. I got busy and rallied support from some of my friends at home, and it looks like construction might finally begin soon. Walt's daughter Diane and I have become good friends, and when I mentioned once that I had never been to Disneyland she practically had a fit. She made me promise that if I ever wanted to come that I would call her and let her handle the accommodations, and you know how I like to keep my word," she said sweetly as she batted her eyes at her daughter.

Jamie just shook her head as she gave her mother an amused smirk. "You are certainly full of surprises today."

"I like to preserve an air of mystery," she replied archly.

They glanced over at Ryan, who was eyeing both of them suspiciously. "Please don't think I'm complaining, but traveling with you two is like being in a foreign country for me. There is nothing about this experience that I'm familiar with."

It was 8:45 when they reached their room, and Caitlin was drooling down Ryan's back as her sleeping head poked out of her sling. They got her changed and placed in the crib, with Ryan sitting next to the bed for a long while, making sure that the child didn't wake.

Catherine decided to read rather than watch a movie, and she was settled comfortably in her navy blue silk pajamas when they were finally ready to leave. "We'll be home by midnight," Jamie promised. "If you get tired, please go to bed, okay?"

"Yes, dear," Catherine nodded obediently.

"No, really, Mom. If Caitlin wakes up you'll hear her, no matter how soundly you sleep."

"I'm not sure that's true," Ryan amended. "Jamie can sleep right through a full scale tantrum."

"You laugh now, Ryan," Catherine said, "but I took her to the doctor because of that when she was small. I thought she was deaf."

"You did?" Jamie asked in shock, never having heard this story.

"I certainly did. We were having some work done on the house in Pebble Beach. You were asleep in your little cradle when one of the workmen dropped an entire pallet of river rocks from a crane. The crane was right outside of your room, and the house shook so hard I thought windows would break. I ran upstairs, and my little princess was still sound asleep. I was relieved until the foreman came up to talk to me and said, 'That's not normal, lady, you'd better make sure she can hear.' I, of course, panicked and took her in the next day, but the doctor assured me that she was just a heavy sleeper, so I stopped worrying."

"Well it looks like I'm going to have to bear all of our children," Ryan said. "If I've got to get up anyway, I might as well be able to nurse them."

"You can be my wet nurse," Jamie teased as she stuck out her tongue. Ryan chased her from the room, pausing to wink at Catherine before she took off.

I've never been attracted to a woman before, but that Ryan O'Flaherty could certainly turn my head if circumstances were different. Jamie never had a chance with that one, she smirked to herself. *Ryan could likely turn the straightest of women gay if she tried hard enough.*

Three hours later they returned to the room, carrying a four-foot-tall stuffed Pluto that Ryan had won at the shooting gallery in the arcade. Catherine was still up, and she gave them an amused smile when she spied their prize. "Should I call the airline for an extra seat?"

"Sure," Ryan said, "but I think he can fly coach. No sense in being extravagant."

She stood the doll up in the corner and said, "I tried to give the darn thing away 20 times. But parents look at you like you're a lunatic when you try to give their kid a toy. I guess I understand their suspicions, but it worries me," she admitted. "I think it's sad that we've over sensitized our kids to potential harm. If I'd tried to give that doll away in Ireland I'd have 20 takers."

"I sure think it's cute," Jamie said, grinning. "And I think it's terribly sweet that you won it for me. She won it with one shot," she informed her mother proudly.

"My Aunt Deirdre's brother is a police officer," Ryan said. "When I was younger, he used to take me to the shooting range on Saturdays. I really enjoyed it. Nice to know I've still got the touch," she said, acting like she was lining up the sights of an imaginary weapon.

"So you had a good time?" Catherine asked.

"We had a fantastic time," Jamie said with a big smile. "We went on seven different rides, and we saw the big light parade and the fireworks. It was really cool."

"Was Caitlin any trouble?" Ryan inquired.

"Not a bit. She didn't make a sound."

"We thought we'd take her over to the park for her breakfast with the characters if you want to sleep in tomorrow," Ryan offered.

"Okay, I'd like that. I'm not much of a morning person," she admitted. "After breakfast you can leave her with me the rest of the day if you wish. I can take her swimming, and I know that will entertain her for a few hours."

"Okay. We'll probably be back here around ten. See you then?"

"Sounds great. Sleep well, you two," Catherine called as she went into her room.

Jamie had been teasing her lover with seductive looks and touches all night long, and once Catherine's door was closed Ryan decided it was payback time. She charged Jamie and scooped her up in her arms, and Jamie's legs instinctively wrapped around her waist. Roughly pushing her up against the door to their room, Ryan began to kiss her deeply, running warm hands all over her body.

The playful teasing quickly turned serious as Jamie joined in and began to escalate the intensity. Her hands went to Ryan's face, holding her tight while she kissed her everywhere, her heart starting to beat wildly. Ryan could feel her partner's pulse throbbing, and she knew that her own heartbeat was racing in tandem. A small, sane part of her told her to stop, but it felt so compelling—so right—that she couldn't get her body to listen.

Their legs grew weak, and slowly but inexorably they began to sink to the floor, having nearly reached it when Catherine started to open her door to clarify a piece of information about their schedule. Luckily, her hearing was quite sharp, and she detected the unmistakable sounds of passion coming from the living room. As quietly as possible, she closed the door without disturbing the young lovers. *I will never, ever open a door on those two again without calling out an alarm.*

"Well, that was…interesting," Jamie observed, picking up her discarded shorts from the floor.

"Too sudden?" Ryan asked solicitously. She placed her fingers under her partner's chin, gently lifting it to be able to look into her eyes.

"No." She spared an impish smile for her partner, crinkling her nose. "I wouldn't like a steady diet of it, though. The carpet burns would likely be a major barrier to my long-term happiness."

Ryan held her at arm's length and carefully assessed her body. "You have an owie?"

"No, you didn't hurt me, but only because we were quick and quiet and tame—for us, that is. I don't want to make a habit of any of those things." She gave Ryan a saucy grin accompanied by wildly waggling eyebrows.

"Lord, I lucked out with you," Ryan decided, tossing Jamie over her shoulder to carry her into their bedroom. Once there, they quietly checked on the blissfully sleeping baby and got ready for bed.

While they snuggled in the big bed, Jamie sighed heavily, and Ryan turned to her and asked, "Want to talk about it?" She placed a few light kisses along her partner's jaw line.

"How do you know what I'm thinking?" Jamie asked, her voice low and laced with amusement.

"I know your sighs. That big one you let out meant, 'I'm worried about my parents.'"

A small chuckle met that assertion. "Hmm…if you really know me that well, I'm in trouble. I'll never have a private thought again."

"It's true," Ryan assured her. "I can see the gears grinding away in there." She tilted her head until she could press her eye right into Jamie's ear. "Yep, there goes another thought." She paused a moment as she deciphered the message. "Hey, I am *not* crazy."

Wrapping her lover in a hug, Jamie murmured, "Well, I'm crazy about you, and I appreciate that you're trying to make me feel better. That means a lot."

"I'm happy to listen if you want to talk. You don't have to censor yourself with me."

"I know, love. I just feel kinda numb right now. I'm trying to summon all my powers of denial until we get back home, since there's not much I can do down here. I want to talk to my father, but I need to do it in person."

"Makes sense. Do you think you can manage to keep the thoughts from intruding?"

"Only with your help. I need to see your sweet face to remind me that everything vital in my life is already within my grasp." She tightened her hold on Ryan's body, emphasizing her point.

"Absolutely true," Ryan whispered. "I will always be here for you."

Caitlin did everyone a favor and not only slept through the night, but also stayed in her crib and quietly played with her new stuffed toys until seven a.m. The blackout curtains made it seem like the middle of the night, and Ryan had not bothered to set her alarm since she assumed the baby would dictate their schedule. Once her eyes had adjusted, Ryan disentangled Jamie's body from hers with some difficulty and crawled out of bed. Leaning over the crib she was greeted by bright green eyes blinking up at her with interest.

"How's my precious one this morning?" Ryan whispered as she lifted her from her little bed.

Caitlin leaned against her bare chest and snuggled in for a long morning cuddle, one of her absolute requirements. She looked around happily as Ryan grabbed what she assumed were her discarded clothes from the night before and struggled to slip her shorts on. The shorts were tough enough, but getting her shirt on and buttoned was no small feat. She managed by shifting the baby from one arm to the other and deciding that all of the buttons weren't strictly required this early in the morning. Grabbing a clean diaper, the pair went out into the living room to rustle up a little breakfast for Caitlin. After heating the bottle under warm water, they sat on the couch snuggling for at least 20 minutes while the milk slowly took the edge off her hunger.

Ryan enjoyed nearly every aspect of being with her cousin, but as they sat together on the couch she decided that this was, by far, her favorite activity. The baby was quiet, almost introspective, in the early morning. The scientist in Ryan knew that Caitlin's busy brain was so frenzied while she slept—building neural pathways and making all sorts of connections—that she needed to adjust a bit in the morning. Cait's brain was basically reordering itself every day, and the potential and promise of her adult self were occurring right before Ryan's eyes. The mere thought of that was overwhelming for Ryan, and she spent a long time stroking the baby's head, daydreaming about the kind of person that Caitlin would grow up to be while the infant sucked rhythmically from her bottle.

Ryan managed to satisfy her own growling stomach by dipping repeatedly into their fruit basket. Quite a while later, Jamie quietly emerged from their room, spying an apple core, the stems from a bunch of grapes and an orange peel all littering the table.

Ryan didn't seem to hear her coming, and she gave a start when Jamie sat down next to her and cuddled up against her side. "You two look so adorable," she murmured, placing a kiss on Ryan's cheek. Caitlin didn't notice that Jamie was in the room, her self-involvement being all-encompassing this morning.

"This is my favorite time with her," Ryan said, bending to kiss Cait's golden head. "Her little brain has been busy all night, and now she's taking in all of the nutrients from her mother's body that she needs to live. I love being able to help her grow."

Jamie had never thought of the process of feeding an infant in quite that way, and she gave her partner a grateful hug for reminding her how special the experience was. "Why does Annie still breastfeed her? Isn't eleven months an awfully long time?"

"No, I don't think so," Ryan said. "There's new research that indicates babies do better the longer they're nursed."

"Isn't there a point at which it's detrimental?" Jamie asked slowly, an image of Ryan breastfeeding their child before her high school graduation leaping into her mind.

"Detrimental? How could it be?"

"Well, I'd think at some point it would hurt the baby's emotional development. I mean, I can't imagine that it's healthy for a three or four-year-old to still be nursing."

"Oh…you mean nursing toddlers." Ryan nodded and said, "I don't know if there's much research on that, but I think a well-adjusted baby eventually weans himself. There comes a point at which they want the independence."

"I take it that you plan on letting our kids make that decision for themselves?"

"Yep," she said decisively. "If they're secure and healthy, they'll stop on their own. Cait's just eleven months, and she's already down to two feedings a day."

"How did Annie produce enough to give us milk for four days? Doesn't her supply diminish when the baby takes less?"

"Yep. But she pumps two or three times a day. She keeps a little supply in the freezer, and she donates the rest at the hospital."

"She what?"

Ryan shot her a look, reminding her that the baby was not in the mood to be startled. "She's a breast milk donor. The best milk is obviously from the mother, but some highly allergic or very ill babies benefit from donated milk. She started doing it as soon as Caitlin started to need less."

"I had no idea," Jamie gaped.

"There's one kid at the hospital who has some rare auto-immune disease. His mother can't produce milk for some reason, and donated milk is the only thing keeping him alive. Annie's been supplying his food for a couple of months now." A fond smile settled onto Ryan's face and she needlessly added, "I'm really proud of her."

"She's a good person," Jamie agreed, having developed quite a bond with the good-natured woman.

Pulling herself from her self-imposed daze, Caitlin beamed up at Jamie and extended her arms, cooing excitedly until Jamie snatched her up and gave her some kisses. Looking over at her grinning lover she remarked, "There is nothing in the world nicer than waking up to your two sweet little faces."

"Well, this little face is still hungry," Ryan decided. "Let's go meet the big dogs."

Chapter Four

A half hour later they were showered and dressed, heading back to the park. Their passports enabled them to enter the park early, so the crush of people was not nearly as bad as it had been the day before. They made their way to Toon Town and found the correct spot for Caitlin's breakfast with Goofy and Pluto. They had their choice of characters, but since her new toys represented the dogs, they thought it made sense to carry out the theme.

"Are we going to tell people that Caitlin isn't ours?" Jamie asked during their walk.

"No need. Young, blonde, green-eyed woman—blonde, green-eyed baby. Everyone will assume she's yours. They won't know what to make of me, but that's okay. I think we should just act normally and let people figure it out."

"It is a little harder when you're a same sex couple, isn't it?" Jamie asked reflectively, thinking that the issue would never come up if Ryan was a man.

"Not if we don't let it be," Ryan said, her confident demeanor carrying Jamie along with her.

They hadn't yet been to Toon Town, and once they arrived Jamie was afraid that she'd never get Ryan into the building where the breakfast was to be held. Ryan was filled with delight, running around the area excitedly as she pointed out all of the sights and whipping Caitlin into a frenzy. *Oh goody*, Jamie thought drolly, *Caitlin will be at her wildest just when we have to sit down to eat*.

After Jamie successfully wrangled the cousins into the building, they found their assigned space, and Jamie was pleased to see that the gathering was very small. There were only about ten other kids and fifteen adults in attendance, but the cacophony of sound in the small, whimsically decorated room belied that fact.

Ryan had been to air shows that seemed quieter, but she did her best to ignore her aversion to noise as she watched Caitlin begin to get into the fun. The room had been set up with small tables and they looked around for one to share, picking one with another baby and her parents. Little Kelsey was two months older than Caitlin, and over the course of the next few minutes Jamie and Ryan were forced to listen to every stellar achievement that the baby had accomplished during her 13 months on the planet. In fact, the child had very well developed verbal skills, and the parents looked at Jamie with some degree of sympathy when she admitted that Caitlin didn't speak yet.

Kelsey's mother, Becky, actually patted Jamie's hand and assured her, "You really shouldn't worry too much that your baby seems a little slow. There's still a chance that she'll catch up."

When Ryan saw the look that flashed in those green eyes, she grabbed a croissant and popped it into Jamie's open mouth. She leaned over and made eye contact with Becky as she said, "Somebody has to be at the bottom of the class. We've just resigned ourselves to the fact that Caitlin will probably have to make a living with her looks." Ryan bit back a howl when Jamie kicked her sharply in the shin, but she wasn't about to get into a contest with these strangers over who had the smartest baby.

Ryan had decided early on that she was never going to bore people to death with tales of Caitlin's development. It wasn't that she didn't think the child was extraordinary—she did. She just firmly believed that perceptive people would pick up on that fact on their own. She didn't have much interest in engaging people who were not perceptive, so she thought the situation would generally resolve itself.

Her comments drew a very startled look from both Becky and her husband Sam, but it didn't stop them from continuing to sing a litany of Kelsey's praises. Ryan was looking around for a sharp knife to impale herself on by the time Goofy and Pluto finally made their appearance and all hell broke loose in the crowded room.

The older kids shrieked and screamed when the big dogs entered the room, and the characters didn't help matters any by running around the room at full speed. Both Caitlin and Kelsey were startled by the noise, as well as the immense size of the animals, and after looking at each other for a moment, both started to scream. Ryan scooped Caitlin up from her high chair and held her on her lap, hugging her tightly until she calmed down. Sam did the same for Kelsey, but it didn't do much good. When Goofy came by the table, Kelsey let out a scream that could easily have broken the sound barrier, and Ryan kicked herself for not bringing earplugs. *Third rule of parenting—always have a pair of earplugs in the diaper bag.* Caitlin snuggled up tightly to Ryan, but when Goofy got down on her level she shyly stuck out her hand and tentatively patted his big black nose, making her cousin beam with pride at her boldness.

Jamie was prepared, and she snapped an adorable photo of the interaction. Caitlin got more and more into the game, and within seconds she held her arms up and Goofy scooped her up from Ryan's lap. A few priceless photos of a delighted baby examining every facet of the huge dog's face commemorated the event. Kelsey was still screaming at an ear splitting decibel level when Goofy handed Caitlin back, and the noise only got worse when

Pluto came sauntering over. Kelsey did everything but crawl into Sam's shirt as she struggled to protect herself from the huge dog, the man finally getting up to take her outside to calm her down.

Much to Ryan's pleasure, Caitlin had no reticence whatever with Pluto. She immediately went to him and giggled wildly when he carried her around the restaurant for a few moments. She kept an eye on Ryan, but managed to have a great time being introduced to the other kids, even slapping hands with the older ones like Ryan had recently taught her. When Pluto handed her back she let out a frustrated cry, her need for stimulation as unquenchable as her older cousin's. Luckily, her attention was quickly diverted when breakfast was served. She happily sat on Jamie's lap and ate almost all of a Mickey shaped waffle, giggling while Jamie made a game of the meal, teasing her playfully.

When Kelsey returned she clung to her mother desperately, unable to eat a bite because of the earlier trauma. Becky opined, "I think the size of the animals confused and frightened her. She's very aware of proportion you know."

"I don't think Caitlin has any idea how big things should be," Ryan said.

"If you don't want your child to be left behind, you'd better start to play games with her to show her progressive sizes and weights of objects," Becky chided, her disapproval obvious.

Ryan had clearly had enough of this nonsense and she dove into one of her favorite pastimes—yanking the chains of pompous people. She slowly scratched her dark head and looked at Becky in confusion. "Play with her?" she asked dully. "You play with her?"

"Of course we play with her and we read stories..."

"Yours can read?" Ryan asked, eyes wide. She turned to Jamie and demanded, "Can ours read?"

"No, I don't think so," Jamie replied, matching the dim-witted tone of her partner. "She's never read to me." She suddenly slapped Ryan on the arm as she recalled, "Ours can't even talk, how could she read?" They both laughed at this for a long while as their tablemates stared at them in astonishment.

Thankfully, breakfast was winding down, and Jamie stood with the baby and bade a pleasant goodbye to their breakfast companions. The best the other couple could do was look from her to Ryan and back again as they mutely nodded.

As soon as they left the building, Jamie pulled Ryan into Minnie's playhouse and laughed until her sides ached. "Yours can read!" she gasped. "Where do you come up with this stuff?"

"I just couldn't stand another minute of listening to them prepare her biography for the Nobel Prize in literature. I figured I could shut them up without being rude. Worked, didn't it?" she asked smugly.

Catherine had eaten and was dressed and ready when they showed up at 10:30. Jamie spent quite a while telling her about their morning exploits while Ryan changed the baby, removing her syrup spattered clothing. "I had no idea you'd be such a tease, Ryan," Catherine said.

"Oh, please," Jamie said. "She's the biggest tease in the world. And she does it with such a straight face that no one ever knows she's kidding."

"I don't think I'm such a tease," Ryan said innocently. "I've always considered myself a torturer." She grabbed Jamie by the hips and lifted her straight up over her head, with Jamie kicking and screaming the whole time. Caitlin was fully used to the rough play of her baby-sitters, and she shrieked for the game to continue. Ryan turned and caught Catherine's open-mouthed look of shock as she winked at her and threatened, "Don't make me mad or you're next."

At one o'clock Catherine and Caitlin were waiting patiently in the big outdoor eating area in Tomorrowland. Caitlin was wearing a brand new outfit that had either been purchased that morning or smuggled in the day before. "Nice clothes, Cait," Ryan said conversationally. "I don't see any mice, dogs, ducks or other animals on them, though. Where'd you get 'em?"

"I had to bring a little something for her, Ryan. I wanted her to have a present."

"Oh, I understand, Catherine," Ryan said, giving her mother-in-law a very composed look of agreement. "A first class airline ticket, a suite in the hotel, and a limo ride are not nearly enough for a one-year-old. I'm afraid you're just going to have to do better."

Catherine's smile disappeared and she said solemnly, "I'll stop if it bothers you. I promise."

"Nope. If you enjoy doing it, go right ahead. I just want you to know that it certainly isn't expected or necessary."

"That's it? No argument?" Catherine asked.

"Nope. I can't ever win with Jamie, and I figure she got her talents from you, so I may as well admit defeat."

"I love a good loser," Catherine said with a smile, sliding her arm around Ryan's waist for a small hug.

As they settled down to eat their fast food, Ryan looked at Jamie with a puzzled frown. "Something's been bothering me all day," she said thoughtfully.

"What is it, honey?"

"Well, Goofy is a dog, right?"

"Yeah, he certainly looks like a dog."

"And Goofy speaks just like Mickey and Minnie do."

"Correct, again. Goofy is verbal."

"But Pluto is Goofy's dog and he doesn't talk. So, are there higher levels of dog? And if not, doesn't that make Pluto a slave of some kind? I mean, subjugating your own species seems like a strange message to give kids."

Smiling fondly at the thoughtful consideration that Ryan had given the problem, Jamie smiled and corrected her theory. "Pluto isn't Goofy's dog. He's Mickey's dog."

"Oh, well, now it makes sense," she said as she crossed her eyes and stuck her tongue out at her lover.

Their discussion was interrupted when Caitlin decided that she was not being fed enough attention or food. Her long wail compelled Jamie to pull her onto her lap, while Ryan cut up tiny bits of a grilled chicken sandwich and popped them into her mouth. Jamie's hands were full of bouncing baby so Ryan cut up bigger bites with bun and condiments for her. She alternated big and little bites gently placed into both smiling mouths while Catherine watched with delight. Ryan occasionally sneaked a little kiss from both blondes as the meal went on, the vast majority of the kisses falling on the smaller blonde's face. It was obvious to even a casual observer that this was a very happy family unit, and no less obvious that the adults were lovers, even though their kisses were brief, infrequent, and chaste.

As Ryan popped another bite into Jamie's mouth she noticed a shadow fall across the table, and she lifted her head to gaze right into the eyes of an extremely angry woman. She sat upright and returned the stare as the woman began to splutter, "Can't you people keep your sickness out of a place like this? It's a crime when a God-fearing country like this can't keep your kind from having children. My little boy shouldn't have to be exposed to perverts like you running around Disneyland."

Ryan shot a warning glance and a quick headshake at Jamie, who was about to get to her feet. Taking a deep breath, Ryan looked up at the shaking woman and calmly asked, "How old is your son?"

That question threw her for such a loop that she responded civilly. She shot a glance at the table she had come from, briefly glancing at her son and husband, both of whom looked like they wanted to dig a hole and hide. "H…he's six," she stuttered.

"And you honestly think the sight of two people expressing their love in a discreet fashion will scar him? I guarantee he didn't notice anything until you pointed it out."

"That's not the point!" she yelled loud enough to cause all of the other diners to turn towards them.

"Sure it is," Ryan said calmly. "He's probably in much more peril from your anger and your hatred of difference than he is from watching people be loving toward one another."

"What you do is sick!" she spat from a few inches in front of Ryan's face.

"Are you a Christian?" Ryan asked, again out of left field.

"Yes, I fear the Lord," she replied haughtily, wielding her faith like a truncheon.

Ryan nodded, drew in a breath and spoke calmly. "I'm no biblical scholar, but I'm sure of one thing. Jesus said that the greatest commandment was to love one another as he loves us." She looked up at the woman and waited for her to disagree. When she received nothing more than a beady-eyed stare she continued. "I'm sure he didn't mean that you have to like what everyone does, but I *am* sure he meant you need to love and accept other people, even when you disagree with them."

"God commands us to reject sin!"

Ryan's eyes narrowed and she allowed some of her anger to show. "If you were really a Christian, you would have approached my family in a much more loving way. I don't want to influence your family with my morals, and I'd appreciate it if you don't infect mine with your hatred." Her anger locked back in place, she gazed up at the woman with a look of total peace and self-assurance, her posture relaxed and open.

Jamie wasn't sure if the woman's blood pressure could withstand the assault. Her face grew even redder as she searched her mind for some comeback—finally throwing her trump card. "Lesbians!" She turned and stalked back to her young son slumping down in his chair and her blank looking husband. Grabbing the boy by the shirt she yanked him to his feet and strode from the eating area, her meek husband following along behind.

Ryan shook her head once as she cut another piece of chicken and offered it up to Caitlin with a smile. The baby had been watching the entire interchange with a concerned look, but she began to smile again as Ryan did. Casting a quick glance at Catherine's horrorstricken face, Ryan asked, "Let's talk about this when Caitlin's down for her nap, okay? I know that was upsetting for you, but I don't want her to pick up on that."

Catherine bit her lip as she quickly gave Ryan a small nod and an even smaller smile. Ryan patted her back and flashed her a grin as she stood, grasping Caitlin in a warm hug and kissing her thoroughly, then she bent and gave her partner a gentle kiss, not willing to let a stranger make her uncomfortable being herself.

Forty-five minutes later they were sitting in their living room with the diaper clad baby. Ryan had spread out a blanket on the floor, and she commenced to place the child in a variety of poses, urging her small muscles to support the growing body in some new ways.

"I'm quite sure I've never seen anyone make a baby exercise before, Ryan," Catherine joked. "Does she belong to a health club?"

"Yep. Cousin Ryan's Private Fitness Training. She's the only member."

"Is that really necessary? I'm sure we didn't do any such thing for Jamie."

"Well, that explains it," Ryan teased, getting a gentle kick to the ribs from her partner. Answering seriously, she said, "I don't think it's a big deal, but I want Caitlin to trust her body and know her capabilities. Getting her used to her muscles and putting some gentle stress on her tendons and bones seems like a good first step."

When the exercise session was finished, Ryan placed the baby on a towel that she had spread out on the sofa and warmed some massage lotion in her hands. Catherine watched as Ryan gave her cousin a thoroughly relaxing massage, working on her tiny back and all four of her little limbs for a long while. Breaking the silence, Catherine asked, "Do you massage her often?"

"Yeah, I do, every chance I get. It makes me feel really connected to touch people like this."

Catherine just shook her head and smiled at the young woman who was so effortlessly working her way into her heart.

After placing Caitlin in her crib, Ryan came back into the sitting room and grabbed a seat on the sofa. They sat, sipping bottled water from the mini-bar until Jamie got up from her chair and went over to sit on Ryan's lap.

"I need a hug," she admitted as Ryan welcomed her. "That incident really upset me."

"Even though you handled it beautifully, I've got to admit that it upset and frightened me," Catherine agreed.

"Tell me what frightened you."

She sat in silence for a moment, trying to put words to her feelings. "I suppose it just made we wish that you didn't have to go through things like that."

"Of course you do," Ryan agreed. "No one would want her child to be harassed like that." Pausing quietly, Ryan asked, "Did it make you wish that Jamie was straight?"

Catherine looked up in shock, feeling that Ryan was reading her mind. She was mightily embarrassed, wishing fervently that she didn't feel that way—but she did, and it was obvious that Ryan sensed it. She nodded her head slowly, a flush traveling up her cheeks.

Ryan gazed at her for a moment, then asked quietly, "Do you ever wish that Jamie was poor, or homely or slow-witted?"

Catherine looked baffled. "No, of course not. But I don't see the analogy."

"I guarantee that if you told a group of people how much money you had, a significant number of them would automatically dislike you because of it. I guarantee that a decent number of people dislike Jamie because of her beauty and her intelligence. But I'm certain that you don't want her to give up those things to please other people. Why not?"

"Because…" she started, but quickly realizing where her mouth was leading her, she firmly clamped her jaw shut.

"Catherine," Ryan began, "please believe that I say this with love. If you want Jamie to change an elemental part of herself to please others, you probably believe that's a part that should be changed. You must believe that it's a part that *you* would change if you could. Otherwise, the wishes of others would seem like what they are—jealousy or ignorance or intolerance."

She gazed at Ryan for a long minute, finally closing her eyes with a sigh. "I don't believe that's true. I just don't want her to be hurt. It hurt so badly to see the look on Jamie's face when that woman started to berate you. Why is it wrong to want to spare her from that?"

"It's not wrong," Ryan reassured her with a gentle smile. "It's every mother's wish to spare her child pain. The difference is that you probably have a small desire to change Jamie to spare her the pain of other people's reactions. What you don't take into account is that that would cause her so much more pain. She is who she is, and trying to be something else is a waste of her gifts. I think you'd have much more peace if you focused on the people who cause her pain, rather than wishing she were different."

"How do I do that?" she asked plaintively.

"Take that woman today," Ryan said. "There are really only three options when you have a situation like that. You can be angry and lash out at her in retaliation, you can see that Jamie stands out in a crowd and be a little angry with Jamie because of it, or you can put the blame where I think it belongs—on people who spout self-righteous nonsense."

Catherine nodded, recognizing the logic of Ryan's words even though she wasn't able to fully let them into her heart.

Ryan continued, "When I refuse to let people influence how I feel about myself, I can look at them with a certain degree of compassion. Can you imagine how horrible it must be to be so filled with rage that you lash out at perfect strangers because they're doing something that bothers you?"

Catherine let her frustration show, looking over at Ryan with wide eyes. "But how do you not let it affect you? She was right in your face saying the most horrible things to you."

"It doesn't affect me because I'm comfortable with who I am," she explained. "I truly believe that my lesbianism is a gift from God. I honestly thank God for making me who I am. That doesn't mean I'm perfect, but I'm the person that God made, and I won't second-guess my maker."

Jamie had been remarkably silent through this whole interchange. She knew that Ryan was on a roll and that her partner was very adept at expressing their mutual feelings on the issue. She also thought that her mother might fare better discussing this with Ryan than with her, perhaps feeling less emotion when discussing it with a third party. Nonetheless, she couldn't help but tighten her hold on her partner, giving her unspoken encouragement for the fine job she was doing.

Catherine was quiet for a few minutes, obviously trying to absorb everything Ryan had said. "So what do I do if you're right? How do I learn to look at this as a gift rather than something I want to change?"

Ryan gave her a wide smile, thinking once again how lucky she was to have this woman for a mother-in-law. "Asking the question provides the answer. If you're open to accepting Jamie for who she is, you will. You just need to spend time with her and you'll become more comfortable over time." She brightened her smile, locking eyes with Catherine as she said, "I don't think you have a long way to go. I've got very good radar when it comes to gay bias, and I don't detect any from you. I think you just need a little time to be able to embrace all of Jamie."

Catherine looked at her daughter, who rested comfortably in Ryan's lap. "You've been awfully quiet. How does all of this affect you?"

"Well," she said, "I'm not at the same place Ryan is on this. My first instinct was to hop up and knock that woman's block off! But I'm getting a lot better at not letting things like this get past my defenses. It helps to live with Gandhi here," she teased, giving her partner a tickle.

Catherine cocked her head at her daughter, asking the question that had been niggling at the back of her brain, "Does it bother you to think I might have some wish that you were different?"

"No, Mom, it really doesn't. You treat both of us very well and you act very comfortable around us. I'd just like you to get more comfortable for yourself."

"So we're doing okay?" she asked hopefully.

"We're doing great," she assured her as she slid off Ryan's lap and sat down on the arm of her mother's chair.

"I just don't want you to be disappointed in me, Jamie," she said softly.

"Mom, I had quite a long period where I fought with my own instincts over this. I knew that I was gay, but I tried everything possible, including a reconciliation with Jack, just so I didn't have to face it. This is hard to get used to, for both of us, but you're doing a fantastic job. I'm happier with our relationship than I have ever been," she said as she enveloped her in a robust hug.

"I am too," Catherine replied softly as a tear escaped from her dark brown eyes.

The insistent beep of her pager caught Ryan's attention and she tracked the device down in their bedroom. "Hmm," she muttered, looking at the number in the display. "That's one of the numbers at school." She fished her wallet out of her back pocket, looking for her calling card.

"Just use the phone, honey," Jamie insisted. "It's okay."

Ryan shrugged and sat down to dial the number. "Hi, this is Ryan O'Flaherty," she announced when the phone was answered with, "Rich Placer's office."

"Oh, hello, Ryan, Coach Placer asked me to call you to let you know that he's had to cancel practice for the rest of the week. He said the next practices will be Monday at ten and four."

"Okay," she said, puzzled by this development. Remembering her manners, she asked, "Coach is okay, isn't he?"

"Oh, yes. There have been some delays in getting the court ready, so there isn't any place to meet this week. That's why he's going to institute double practices next week."

"Oh, goody," Ryan said unenthusiastically, remembering how drained the two-a-days in Santa Cruz had left her.

"I'll give him the message," the woman said, chuckling a little as she hung up.

"Trouble?" Jamie asked.

"Not really." She paused for a moment and said, "Actually, I guess it was good news. I have the rest of the week off. We don't start practice until Monday."

"Cool. Can we stay later tomorrow, Mom?"

"Of course. I don't have any need to hurry home. We can stay another night if you wish."

"Mmm…I think Caitlin might be ready to head home tomorrow," Ryan decided. "Besides, we'll be out of milk by then, and I don't want to have to switch to formula."

"Is it okay if we leave late in the day?" Jamie persisted.

"Yep. We've got five bottles left. That will get us through dinner tomorrow."

"Cool," Jamie said, obviously not in the mood to leave their playground. "I'll get on the phone and see if we can change our flight."

After Caitlin woke from her nap Ryan changed her and brought her in to sit with the grownups while she acclimated. She cuddled up in a little ball as she sank against Ryan's chest with a contented sigh, still halfway between wakefulness and slumber.

Catherine shared an affectionate smile with her daughter as they watched Ryan comfort and coo to the small child.

"She does have a certain presence," mother observed to daughter, shaking her head.

"More like a gravitational pull," Jamie corrected her as she walked over to the chair and struggled to find room to share. Ryan gladly shifted a little to allow her partner to climb aboard, and the three of them shared a warm group hug for a few minutes. "Sing her favorite song, honey," Jamie urged, always loving to hear her partner's voice.

Ryan grinned at her, knowing she was being set up, but not caring a bit. She cuddled the baby close to her chest so she could feel the vibrations of the music through her body. She usually sang the song with a great deal of vigor, but she wanted Caitlin to wake slowly, so she softened her voice and sang it with a slow, gentle beat.

Oh! My boat can safely float in the teeth of wind and weather
And outrace the fastest hooker between Galway and Kinsale;
When the black floor of the ocean and the white foam rush together,
High she rides, in her pride, like a sea gull through the gale.
Oh she's neat! Oh she's sweet! She's a beauty in ev'ry line!
The Queen of Connemara is that bounding barque of mine.

When she's loaded down with fish till the water lips the gunwale,
Not a drop she'll take on board her that would wash a fly away;
From the fleet she'll slip out swiftly like a greyhound from her kennel,
And she'll land her silver store the first at ould Kinvara quay.
Oh she's neat! Oh she's sweet! She's a beauty in ev'ry line!
The Queen of Connemara is that bounding barque of mine.

There's a light shines out afar, and it keeps me from dismaying
When the skies are ink above us and the sea runs white with foam,
In a cot in Connemara there's a wife and wee one praying

To the One who walked the waters once, to send us safely home.
Oh she's neat! Oh she's sweet! She's a beauty in ev'ry line!
The Queen of Connemara is that bounding barque of mine.

The baby's small body rocked in time to the music, her little foot rapping against Ryan's leg. She had a dreamy expression on her small face and her eyes were largely unfocused, seemingly transported to some distant place by the deep melodic voice and the warm hug she was wrapped in.

Catherine watched transfixed as the family of choice snuggled together, their bodies molded together as if they shared the same skin. Once again, deep pangs of regret washed over her for missing out on moments like this, but she did her best to keep her promise and focus on the present and the future. "You have a beautiful voice," she said softly, not wanting to disturb the trance that Caitlin seemed to have fallen into.

"Thanks," Ryan said. "My grandfather used to sing that song to me when we went out on his boat." She laughed softly and said, "I have dozens of songs that I remember singing with him when I was small, but nearly every one ends with the sailor being lost at sea, and his wife standing at the shore cursing the waves."

Blinking slowly, Catherine asked, "Why were the songs so sad?"

"That's just the way people experienced life," she said, shrugging her shoulders. "The ocean is a dangerous place."

"My father was a sailor, too," Catherine said, a look of infinite sadness stealing over her features.

Ryan gazed at her quietly for a moment and said, "I guess you could technically call my grandfather a sailor, but I think of him as a fisherman."

"Ahh," Catherine said, recognizing the difference. "He made his living that way?"

"Yes. I'm not sure how many generations of Ryans have made their living on the sea, but it's more than a few." She gave Catherine a small smile and said, "I suppose the tradition will die with my grandfather."

"That's rather sad," Catherine said.

"Yes, in a way it is, but it's a hard, dangerous way to make a living. The romance of the lure of the sea is mostly fantasy. Not many people fish for their livelihood if they have other options."

Catherine just nodded, spending a moment trying to imagine how vast the differences were between her family and Ryan's, and how ill-equipped her family members would be to live a life of manual labor. For just a moment she let her imagination wander and realized that Ryan's working-class family would be just as ill-equipped to live a life of leisure. *I wonder who would acclimate quicker?*

After a few moments, Caitlin began to stir, indicating her readiness to begin her usual enthusiastic activities. After a brief discussion, they decided to go down to the pool together rather than head back to the park, the adults reasoning that there would be much shorter lines after the majority of the families had left for the day.

Caitlin, of course, wore her new Mickey suit, and when they were ready they slogged all of their gear down to the pool. Catherine wore a very becoming straw hat and a plain but very attractive white sundress, appearing to all a young mother carrying her adorable baby.

The new Neverland pool had opened earlier in the summer, and it was obviously the place to be on this warm afternoon. The hotel complex held two other pools, but they were both shunned by the patrons who wanted to sample the more elaborate play area.

The irregularly shaped pool area was quite large. A lengthy water slide was tucked into a tall group of boulders, and Jamie rolled her eyes when she realized that her partner would likely be on the slide all afternoon.

They managed to find three lounge chairs in the shade of a grouping of small palm trees planted in giant containers. They had all applied sun block to each other before they left the room, but just to make sure she was protected Ryan tugged a long sleeved T-shirt onto the baby after allowing the official photographer to snap a few shots of her posing in her new suit. The tot also had on her new yellow hat, giving extra warmth to her already sunny face.

After Caitlin was settled, Ryan handed the baby to her mother-in-law so she could remove her own clothing. The sun was behind Ryan's back, and as she grinned down at Caitlin she pulled off her T-shirt, completely exposing her body to Catherine's gaze for the first time. She wore her usual suit, which consisted of a tight white sports bra and navy blue high-cut bottoms. But there was nothing usual about the way the suit clung to every curve, highlighting the generous swell of her breasts as well as the graceful curve of her hips.

Catherine tried to avoid staring, but she was not having an easy time of it. After Ryan kicked off her shorts, she stood up tall and began to stretch her arms in a windmill motion, loosening them up before she stressed them. As Catherine stole another glance she was stunned to see that even though the bulk of the sun was obscured by Ryan's body, the rays radiated around her like a golden aura. Her powerful and remarkably feminine body was displayed beautifully by the gleaming sunlight, and the thought crossed Catherine's mind that the scene reminded her of the birth of Venus.

Catherine was still staring when Ryan extended her hands and said, "Want me to take her?"

"Huh?" Catherine gaped, not sure of the question.

"Want me to take the baby?" Ryan answered patiently, recognizing the look for exactly what it was.

Catherine extended her arms, blinking slowly as Ryan grinned and took the baby into the pool. Turning to look at her daughter with a totally blank face, Catherine shook her head to clear it. Jamie smiled and remarked, "Don't you wonder why I ever let her out of the house?"

Catherine mutely nodded as she looked toward the pool to order her thoughts. But that didn't help a bit, since Ryan was cavorting in the pool with the baby, displaying her flawless body as she moved about gracefully in the water. Catherine finally managed to get out, "I…I…don't think I've ever seen a woman who looks like that."

Jamie spent a moment looking at Ryan from her mother's frame of reference. She decided that most of her mother's friends looked exactly alike. Most of them were small, under 5'6" or so, and all of them were thin. But when Jamie really thought about it, she realized that they were not just thin, they were emaciated. She knew that her mother weighed less than 100 pounds, and she guessed that her friends were the same. Many of them belonged to a gym or had one at home, but even though their bodies were toned, none of them had an ounce of noticeable muscle.

"Those muscles," Catherine mumbled. As she said that, it dawned on Jamie that her mother's gaping had less to do with Ryan's looks than with her sturdy body.

"Well, part of it is just great genes, but she also had to look great to have credibility as a personal trainer. I can only assume she'll get in even better shape by playing volleyball. At least I hope she will," she admitted with a chuckle. "I hate to be so shallow, but that is too valuable a natural resource to waste."

"I should say so," Catherine agreed weakly, never taking her eyes off the remarkably well-built young woman playing in the pool.

Jamie hopped into the water to join Ryan, sidling up to her with a chuckle. "Mother's mouth is still hanging open, honey. Maybe you should have worn a T-shirt."

Ryan smiled as she acknowledged, "I saw the look. I'd forgotten that she'd never really seen me before. I guess I'm not the normal Hillsborough matron, huh?"

"I think you could safely say that most of her friends don't resemble you in any way."

"Maybe we should move down there and I'll set up my personal training business. Your mom could send all of her friends—I'd have a built-in client base."

"Mother is doing great at accepting us, honey, but let's not get loony."

After they had played in the water for a while, Ryan grew too hungry to continue. Catherine called over a waiter and insisted that Ryan order something. She relented and got a chocolate malt to tide her over. When it was delivered, Catherine looked at Ryan with envy as she confessed, "I don't think I've had a chocolate malt since I was a child."

Ryan gave her a puzzled glance. "Why not?"

"Goodness, Ryan, there must be a thousand calories in that," she said, laughing, as though that declaration explained everything.

Ryan held up the Styrofoam cup and regarded it carefully. She pursed her lips and shook her head as she said, "No…this one is more like 1,500 calories. There was a lot of whipped cream on top that I stirred in."

"That's more than I consume in a day. Much more, as a matter of fact."

Ryan's eyes grew wide. "No wonder you're just skin and bones. You can't enjoy life on a starvation diet."

"But it's what I'm used to," she insisted, a little defensively.

"That's probably because your metabolism has slowed down so much. It thinks you're being starved, and it slows down to conserve resources." She regarded Catherine for a few moments. "Would you be interested in working out with me? I could help kick your metabolism into gear so you could eat like normal people and help you put some muscle on."

"Is it really necessary to have visible muscles?" she asked tentatively, not wanting to insult either of her companions.

"You don't need as much as I do since you wouldn't want to compete in sports, but having muscle really helps as you age. It keeps you much younger looking and helps prevent osteoporosis."

"Okay, Ryan," she said decisively, "you're on. Where do we start?"

"We start by you helping me drink this malt," she said with a smile as she held the cup out.

Catherine looked reticent but she gamely accepted and took a long swallow. "Oh, my God," she moaned closing her eyes in pleasure, "I had forgotten how good ice cream could taste."

"Stick with me, Catherine. I'll reintroduce you to every guilty pleasure you've denied yourself."

Jim will throw a fit when he hears this, both women thought silently.

Refreshed, they resumed their games until the sun was fully behind the hotel and the air began to chill slightly. Even though she was cold, Caitlin had no desire to leave her little paradise. She began to wail when Ryan removed her from the pool, so Ryan wrapped her in a big towel and carried her to a quieter part of the pool. Jamie got up and offered a bottle, but Ryan declined, saying, "I don't think she's hungry, and I hate to comfort her through food. She needs to know that she can get over her heartaches on her own."

After ten solid minutes of screaming Ryan finally realized that she was torturing the child by walking around the pool area—keeping the object of Caitlin's desire in front of her. Signaling to Jamie, she left the pool and wandered around, finally happening upon a two-story water feature.

A long, winding set of stairs led to a walkway that was below grade, with a large waterfall breaking all around. The noise was intense, just intense enough that Caitlin's cries couldn't be heard by the other guests. Now the baby wanted to be released so that she could get into the waterfall, and Ryan had no doubt that she would do so if she let her. *Dear Lord, please don't make our kids as wild as Caitlin. She just has no fear.* Pausing for a minute, she had to acknowledge, *How do you think Da felt trying to keep control of you?*

It took another fifteen minutes of constant wailing for Caitlin to finally cry herself out, and by this time Ryan's head was throbbing. Her companions had abandoned the pool, and as they passed it, Caitlin let out another few pathetic moans, kicking frantically to be released, but Ryan held firm, knowing that the baby had to learn that sometimes she couldn't have what she wanted.

Caitlin threw herself at Jamie when the hotel room door opened. The little face was red and streaked with tears, her breathing still choked from emotion. Jamie gave Ryan a concerned look as the baby turned her face from Ryan, refusing to even look at the traitor. "Boy, she's really pissed off."

"Oh yeah," Ryan agreed. "She's not on my top ten list at the moment either. Mind if I take a nap? My head's about to explode."

"Go right ahead, honey. We'll watch her." As Ryan trudged into their room, Jamie asked, "Do you have anything you'd like to do for dinner? We probably need to make reservations."

"No noise, no kids," Ryan decreed, closing the door firmly behind her.

"Well, that should be easy to find at Disneyland," Jamie said, smiling at her mother. "Any ideas?"

"Of course. I'm full of ideas."

Chapter Five

"You know," Catherine said as she rocked Caitlin in her arms, "it makes me feel better to see that even Ryan has her moments when the baby is too much for her."

"It hasn't happened since I've known her," Jamie said, "but then, we've never had her for this long, either. Annie is even more patient than Ryan, and she's told me that sometimes she wants to put her in her crib and close the door for a few hours. I think this is really good for us," she said reflectively. "I'd been thinking that it might be nice to have a baby next year, but this is making me re-think that."

Catherine's eyes fluttered closed, and before she could censor herself she said, "Oh, Jamie, please don't do that."

"Don't do what, have a child, or wait?"

Catherine shook her head briskly, angry with herself for butting into her daughter's business. "I'm sorry. I shouldn't try to force my opinions on you."

"No, Mom, I want your opinion. This is important."

Catherine took a deep breath, trying to decide how much of her feelings to reveal. "I...I don't think it's wise to have a child so soon."

"I know it was hard for you, Mom," Jamie acknowledged, "but things will be easier for us. We've got a really good support system with Ryan's family, and I know you'll be there for us."

Catherine nodded, smiling fondly at her daughter for knowing that she would support her in any way possible. "I'm sure you're right. I'm just being silly."

There was a long, uncomfortable silence as Jamie tried to discern the hidden cause of her mother's concern. She finally asked, "You're not worried about the baby part, are you?"

The silence continued for a few more moments. "Not entirely," Catherine admitted.

"What is it? Come on, level with me."

Catherine shook her head, not wanting to be drawn into this discussion. "Jamie, I spoke out of turn. I have my own projections that I'm putting onto you, and it's not fair. I'm sure you and Ryan will do what's right for you."

Not buying the brush-off, Jamie persisted. "Why won't you be honest with me? I thought we trusted each other?"

She was clearly hurt, and Catherine once again regretted bringing up the subject. "All right, dear. I uh…I don't know how to say this delicately, so I'll just say it." She took a deep breath, and looked down at the baby, seemingly afraid to meet her daughter's eyes. "You've told me that Ryan's been with a lot of other women."

"Yeah," Jamie said, puzzled at the direction of the conversation.

"I think it might be a good idea to see how she adjusts to monogamy before you decide to have children together."

All at once, it all became clear to Jamie. She knew why her parents treated each other so coolly; she knew why her mother could be gone for months at a time without any qualms; she knew why she never saw her parents kiss or display any physical affection. All of these thoughts flashed in her mind so quickly that her face twitched and contorted as she was bombarded with the images.

Catherine saw the tumult on her daughter's face and misinterpreted it. "I'm sorry for saying that. I certainly don't think badly of Ryan. I just...I've seen so many of my friends..."

Jamie cut her off, looking at her with deep compassion. "When was the first time?" she asked softly.

"The first time?" Catherine asked, not understanding the question.

"When did Daddy start having affairs?" she asked again, making her question plainer.

Catherine blanched, clutching at the neckline of her dress with a shaking hand. "I didn't say that to imply...," she began, but her determined daughter cut her off again.

"It's obvious, Mom. I should have seen it years ago. When did it start?" Her voice was quiet, but firm, and Catherine could feel the love and support pouring from her daughter, encouraging her to speak the truth.

Strangely, at the last minute she pulled back and said, "Jamie, every marriage has problems, and we've had our share. I just don't think it wise to burden you with them. Please, let us have our secrets."

"It's okay, Mom. It's obvious that Daddy's been unfaithful."

Catherine held her ground. She knew that Jamie and her father had a difficult road ahead, and she had no intention of making that path any more arduous than it had to be. Jamie could have her suspicions, but Catherine was not going to be the one to confirm them to her daughter. "No, honey," she said gently. "Both of us have made mistakes in our marriage. We've hurt each other deeply. But that doesn't give me the right to talk about him behind his back. I made a vow that I would honor our relationship, and talking about things like this is not very honorable."

Jamie nodded, perversely pleased that her mother would not reveal her troubles. She knew in her soul that her father had been unfaithful—she could see it written in the bold emotions that flashed across her mother's face—but she was filled with new respect for the woman for keeping his secrets. "I won't ask again," she said softly. Rising from her chair she crouched down in front of her mother and leveled her gaze. "Thank you for never letting me see the trouble you were having. It was awfully nice to grow up in an intact family."

"You've always been our first concern, Jamie," Catherine said, wrapping an arm around her daughter.

"Do you have someone you can confide in, Mom?" she asked softly, not able to bear her mother dealing with her hurts alone.

"Two hundred dollars an hour buys a very good listener," Catherine joked, some of her normal wry humor returning to her voice.

Ryan emerged from their room at seven, her sleep-creased face and nearly-shut eyes reflecting very recent awakening. She stood in the doorway scratching her head, looking like she didn't know what direction to travel in.

"Come here, love," Jamie urged, patting the cushion next to her. Catherine was sitting on the floor with the baby, both of them intently watching The Little Mermaid on the Disney Channel. Ryan shuffled over to the couch, her feet never leaving the carpet. Folding her long frame onto the available space, she draped her legs over the arm of the sofa, resting her head in Jamie's lap.

As skillful fingers began to rub her scalp, Ryan warned, "I'll be out in moments if you keep that up."

"That's fine," Jamie urged. "Go back to sleep, sweetheart. We're having dinner delivered. Sleep 'til it gets here."

Without a word of protest the broad chest began to rise and fall slowly, closed eyes darting rapidly under long-lashed lids.

A quiet rap on the door caused Ryan's eyes to pop open a half-hour later. Alert blue orbs scanned the room, fixing everyone's position as Catherine got up to answer. Ryan sat up as the door opened to a man carrying two large grocery bags.

Turning to her partner, Ryan asked, "'Webvan.com' down here? Without a computer?"

"No," Jamie said. "We had to do this the old-fashioned way. Via the telephone."

The man set the bags on the table, happily accepting the money that Catherine handed him. He counted it aloud as he moved to the door, turning to give her a pleasant smile as he determined how much his tip was. "Call any time!" he said brightly.

"What was that all about?" Ryan asked, going to the bags to watch Catherine unpack.

"We thought it would be nice to have dinner brought to us," Catherine said. "So I asked the concierge for the name of the best grocery store in Orange County. I spoke with the manager of the store, we made the arrangements, he called a cab, and here we are."

She said this all so matter-of-factly that Ryan had to laugh. "I bet it was a little harder than that, Catherine."

"Only a little," she insisted. "They were really quite accommodating."

"I just bet they were," Ryan commented wryly, knowing that money talked.

Over some fabulous duck raviolis they discussed their plans for the remainder of their trip. "I need to go on some roller coasters," Ryan stated.

"Go over tonight," Catherine said. "You can put Caitlin to bed and stay until they close, since you had such a good nap."

"Done," Ryan decreed. "Now, since the baby hasn't really seen the park, maybe we should take her over tomorrow for early admission and let her explore Toon Town. Then we could go on a couple of kiddie rides and come back for her nap."

"That sounds good," Jamie agreed. "What do you think, Mom?"

"That's fine, girls. I think she should go on some type of ride on her first visit."

"What about you, Catherine?" Ryan drawled. "This is your first trip to Disneyland…shouldn't *you* go on something?"

She looked a bit taken aback as she considered the notion. "I…I…I wouldn't know what to go on. I've never been to an amusement park."

"Never? Not one?"

"No, I'm fairly certain that I would remember if I had."

"Jeez, who says rich people have all the fun?!" Ryan asked as she let out an exasperated breath.

As soon as they reached the lobby, Ryan directed Jamie away from the monorail, leading her to one of the deserted pools. She sat on a chaise and pulled her partner down with her, saying, "You're as tense as a python, love. I could tell you were putting on a good front, but you don't have to do that around me. Tell me what's going on."

Sighing heavily, Jamie leaned back against her partner, immediately feeling a little better just to be able to vent. "Don't leave me alone with Mother anymore," she moaned.

"What? I thought you were enjoying being alone with her."

With a bitter laugh Jamie said, “I enjoy everything but the revelations she keeps dropping on me. I don’t think I can take much more,” she said softly.

Beginning to massage the tense muscles in her partner’s shoulders, Ryan asked, “What now, honey?”

“My father had an affair.” Jamie’s voice was flat, but Ryan could feel the torrent of emotion that was poorly hidden by her tone.

Unconsciously, Ryan’s hands stilled as the weight of the secret she carried settled onto her shoulders. She had put more thought and spent more time worrying about this issue than she had invested on her decision on where to attend graduate school.

In her heart, she knew that Jamie would want to know about her father’s indiscretion, but she was just as confident that it would have done no good to tell her. She knew that telling would severely harm Jamie’s relationship with her father, and she had a real fear that having the secret out in the open could destabilize the Evans’ marriage.

Even though it was incredibly hard for her to keep this knowledge to herself, she still thought it was the correct decision. Over time, she had developed a well-thought-out code that she tried to never vary from. That code dictated that she never reveal secrets about a living person unless she could spare someone else pain by doing so.

When the incident with Jim had first occurred, Ryan had been tormented about what to do. Finally deciding that she needed to stick to her beliefs, even though she knew Jamie would be unhappy about it, she had been able to put the issue aside for the most part. Now, however, she tried to still her heart, knowing that she had to reveal what she knew now that the secret was out.

Jamie continued, "I don't know if this is something that happened a long time ago or if it's still going on, but the whole thing sickens me," she said, leaning hard into Ryan's body.

Oh, shit! Well, that clinches it. She doesn't know much—Catherine might not even know that it's still going on. If it made sense to keep the damn secret before, it still does now.

The tense body in her arms moved slowly, as Jamie's head swiveled around so that she could look into Ryan's eyes. "You aren't surprised," she said slowly. It wasn't a question, it was a statement, and she cocked her head quizzically, seeking confirmation.

In an instant, Ryan had to make her decision. Pursing her lips, she decided to follow her conscience and not reveal what she knew. "I'm not surprised, Jamie," she said softly, her eyes blinking slowly. "I uh…I think it's pretty darned common for powerful people to cheat. I read a survey once that showed there was a very high correlation among wealth, power and cheating."

Satisfied with her answer, Jamie turned and cuddled into Ryan's body once again. "I don't care if every other man in America does it," she said, her anger just below the surface of her still-calm voice. "It sickens me, Ryan. I'll never be able to respect him again."

Resuming her massage, Ryan urged, "Please don't say that, honey. I know that you're angry, but it's really hard to look at someone's marriage and assign blame. That's really between your parents."

"You didn't see her eyes," she said softly, a few tears starting to fall. "You didn't see the hurt."

"No, I didn't." Ryan leaned over to kiss Jamie's head. "I'm really sorry that your mom had to go through that. I can't imagine how much that would hurt." Still stroking her back, Ryan stated one more time, "Even though it's a horrible thing for your mom,

I still think you have to let it be between them. This isn't your fight, and I can't imagine that your mom wants you to fight her battles for her."

Jamie sat up and gazed at her partner for a moment, the look so intent that Ryan began to pull back from it. "Don't *you* think this is disgusting? Aren't *you* furious with him?"

Ryan pursed her lips and shook her head. "If your dad cheated on your mom without her knowledge or permission—of course I'm angry with him. But I don't know what happened between them, babe. It's really none of my business, and I don't want to take sides or assign blame when I don't know all of the facts."

With another heavy sigh, Jamie scooted around until she could face her partner. "Ryan," she said softly, her voice full of emotion. "I don't understand why you're not outraged, but I certainly hope it's not because you think cheating isn't a big deal."

Ryan's eyes went so wide they almost hurt. Before she could get a word out, Jamie cut her off by pressing her fingertips to her lips. "I know this seems like something that could never happen to us, but some day, after we've been together for a while, you might be tempted."

Once again Ryan started to interrupt, to defend herself against the mere suggestion that she could ever be unfaithful, but Jamie silenced her once again. "Hear me out, please," she begged.

Ryan nodded silently.

"I just want you to know that to me, cheating is an unforgivable sin. As much as I love you—and I love you more than I can say—I will not tolerate it—in any form. That is the only thing that would ever make me leave you, Ryan. I would leave you…as hard as that is to conceive…if you were ever intimate with another woman."

Tears were welling up in Ryan's eyes and Jamie gently wiped them away with the tips of her fingers, leaning forward to kiss each soft eyelid.

"I know that sounds harsh, sweetheart, but I feel so strongly about this that I need to tell you. I don't ever want there to be any misunderstanding about this."

"I understand," Ryan whispered, her voice rough with emotion. "I know that it's easy to promise my fidelity now, Jamie, when things are so new and exciting, but I swear with every fiber of my being that I will never betray our love."

"That's it, baby," she said softly. "It's the betrayal. People think it's about sex, but it isn't. It's betrayal. I'm glad that you understand that."

"I do," Ryan vowed, holding her beloved close, and wishing that she could erase the hurt that was so evident on her face.

After holding each other and talking softly in the warm night, they decided to go back to the park and try to put the upsetting topic to rest for a while. Jamie mused that it was really fortuitous that they were in a place where the entire culture revolved around carrying people into a fantasy. After just a few minutes they got into the spirit and managed to have a good time, even with all of the turmoil of the evening.

At 11:30 they finally reached the entrance to Space Mountain. They had managed to get on every other attraction that caught their interest, but every time they had come by this one, the line had been too long. By 11:15 the estimated time was down to 20 minutes, so they hopped in line.

Jamie was a little apprehensive as they waited. She had been to a big amusement park in Santa Clara when she was in high school, but she had been too afraid to go on any of the roller coasters. She was dating a rather wild boy at the time and she knew he would make the experience more frightening than normal, so she wisely stayed on the ground and held everyone's change and wallets.

She wasn't generally afraid of heights or falling, and speed wasn't an unpleasant sensation either, so she assumed she would like the ride as long as she had Ryan with her, but still she felt a little gripping in her stomach.

Ryan, of course, was bubbling with excitement. She loved all things fast, and she had to admit that roller coasters were one of her favorite guilty pleasures. Her arms were draped around Jamie's shoulders from behind, and as they got closer, she could tell that her lover was trembling slightly. Leaning over, she whispered into her ear, "It's okay to feel a little nervous. That can actually make it more fun."

Jamie turned and shot her a doubtful glance, but Ryan persisted. "I'm certain that this ride is completely safe. I'll have my arms around you the entire time. I won't let anything bad happen to you."

Jamie nodded quickly as she tried to take a few deep breaths. As they got closer, Ryan did the math and figured out that they would be in the last car of the ride. Releasing Jamie, she walked back through the line until she got to two young men. She spoke to them for a moment and signaled to Jamie to come back to join her as the young men switched places with her. "What was that all about?" she asked.

"We were going to be in the last car. I like it back there, but it's very whippy. I thought it might be too rough for you, so I switched places so we'd be right in the middle. That's where you get the smoothest ride," she promised, bending to kiss Jamie's nose.

"You take such good care of me," Jamie mumbled as she snuggled her face into Ryan's shirt.

Moments later they were herded aboard the capsule that would be their home for the next three minutes. The pod held eight cars, and Ryan quickly directed Jamie to sit in the third sone. She got in next to her and scooted over until she was tight against her body, the bar lowered to hold them in. She snaked one long arm around Jamie's back and under her right arm, resting her hand firmly around her partner's waist.

They were immediately plunged into complete darkness and Jamie felt her stomach do a little flip, but Ryan's arm tightened a bit and she felt the tension ease. Nevertheless, she slid her hand between Ryan's legs and tightly wrapped her arm around a thigh just for added protection.

It was obvious that they were climbing, but it was not clear how steep the angle was. She began to observe how vital a role sight played in spatial orientation, but just as the observation was formed in her mind, the car began to drop. It seemed that they were falling off a cliff at a 90-degree angle, but she knew that wasn't possible. Even so, it was hard to convince her inner gyroscope, especially since she was basically blind. There were tiny little lights representing stars up on the ceiling and walls, but they provided no illumination in the utter blackness. Just when she thought they would surely crash to the ground, the car made an abrupt right turn and they were catapulted forward with a whipping motion.

As the car began to make a series of tight, banked curves, she heard a piercing scream—only to discover that the voice was her own. Another quick climb had her braced for the worst as she grabbed Ryan so hard she was afraid she would pull her leg from the socket. But this drop was much less severe than the previous one and she began to relax, only to scream again as they dipped quickly at least four times, each time a little deeper. One last tightly banked loop around the structure, and the car slid to a stop at the dimly lit platform.

She looked over at Ryan with profound relief on her face. "My throat hurts," she said with a little puppy dog look.

"How do you think my ear feels?" Ryan gently teased as she exited and held out a hand to assist her. "Come to think of it, my right leg is numb, too. I should be more afraid of you than I am of the ride."

Jamie leaned against her as they exited the building. "Even though I was scared spitless, that was kind of a rush," she said with a grin. "Can we go again tomorrow?"

"Yet one more example of what I love about you," Ryan beamed with pride.

"Wanna sit by the pool for a while?" Jamie asked as they approached the hotel.

"Bet it's locked," Ryan accurately guessed. "Not ready to go inside?"

Jamie shrugged, looking like she was uncertain. "No, it's not that," she said. "I just want a few minutes alone with you. Even though the baby's asleep, I still notice that she's there." She looked up at Ryan with a clear hint of desire in her eyes. "I'm still a little wired up from the roller coaster," she admitted. "It got my blood pumping."

Ryan had an immediate desire to pinch a few places where she guessed the blood was pumping particularly strongly, but she behaved herself since they were in a public place. "Let me show you a little spot I discovered when I was walking Caitlin around earlier," she suggested, taking Jamie's hand.

They walked down the ramp to the below-ground waterfalls. The falls provided a very soothing background noise to the resort, giving the place an almost tropical flavor. "This is cool!" Jamie said, having to increase her volume so that Ryan could hear.

"Cait liked it," Ryan agreed. "She wanted to jump in, of course."

"Mmm…I don't have that desire."

"What desire do you have?" Ryan asked, pressing her body against her partner's back. Her head dropped a bit and she started to nibble on the soft skin of Jamie's neck, nuzzling the shirt away from her skin to get more access.

Jamie's hands slid behind Ryan pulling her in tighter. Twitching her hips a few times she turned her head and said, "I think we've done this enough to have you recognize the signs, Tiger. Think hard."

"That's always so hard to do when your body's moving against mine," Ryan said, not kidding in the least. "As soon as you start to touch me, my brain takes a break. The hotter I get, the dumber I get. We're gonna have to start making love less, or I might flunk out of school."

Jamie turned around and wrapped her arms around Ryan's neck, pulling her down for a soft kiss. "I'll admit that you do tend to act rather than think when we're intimate, but the phenomenon seems to be short-lived. You seem perfectly lucid when you're vertical."

"Not so," Ryan grinned, "I'm vertical now, and I bet you could render me as dumb as a box of rocks with very little effort."

"Hey!" Jamie teased. "Don't demean my skills. It takes a lot of work to drive that massive intellect down to the amoeba-like level it sometimes falls to. How about a little respect?"

Ryan linked her hands behind the small of her partner's back, letting a stray finger or two roam a little lower. "I have nothing but respect for your skills, sweetheart. No one has ever rendered me stupider than you have."

"Aww…you say the sweetest things." Jamie grinned, and stood on her tiptoes to kiss her partner. The kiss lasted a little longer than she had planned, and soon Ryan's hands were splayed out across her butt, squeezing her cheeks with abandon.

"I've already lost my ability to perform quadratic equations," Ryan murmured. "Polynomials are next. Heeeeeelp."

"Come on, hot stuff," Jamie chuckled. "Let's get upstairs while you can still remember how to walk."

"I don't think I can do this," Jamie whispered to her partner. The sheet, blanket and comforter were pulled over their heads to provide not only privacy, but a small sound barrier.

"It is a little close in here," Ryan agreed.

"No, not that," she whispered. "I don't think I can stay quiet enough. You get dumb, but I get loud."

Running her fingers down her partner's face, Ryan said. "I always knew you'd be hot in bed. I just had no idea you were so…vocal," she said, trying to be as diplomatic as possible.

"You can say it," Jamie smirked. "I'm a screamer. No two ways around it."

"That's not a bad thing," Ryan said. "It's nice to get such clear feedback on my work. It's like getting your grade report right when you're finishing your final answer."

Even though it was pitch black under the covers, Jamie found and patted her lover's cheek affectionately. "You're Summa Cum Laude in my book, Tiger. I just don't think I can keep my opinion to myself, though. I've never tried to be quiet."

"We certainly don't have to do this if you don't want to. You know that I never want you to be uncomfortable."

"Oh, it doesn't make me uncomfortable," Jamie decided. "I honestly don't know if I can do it, though. I don't want to traumatize Caitlin."

"Honey," Ryan reminded her, "she's eleven months old. She has no idea what we're doing—except that it would look like we're having fun. You know you spend half of our lovemaking giggling, and that certainly wouldn't frighten her."

Jamie chuckled at Ryan's slight exaggeration and said, "Yeah, but I spend the rest of the time crying, 'Oh God! Oh God!'"

"She'll think we're just saying our prayers," Ryan said, grinning. "Again, I don't want to pressure you, but she won't know a thing, even if we do wake her up. We just have to be prepared to stop if she does wake."

"Stop?" Jamie raised an eyebrow, but it was too dark for her partner to see it. "Oh, no, no stopping. Once the train leaves the station we've got to get to the next stop." She was chuckling as she said this, the low sound making Ryan smile in response.

Giving her a hug, Ryan said, "You might just have to go into the bath to bring the train home, but I still think it's worth the trip."

After a short pause to make up her mind, Jamie sighed and said, "All right, I'm game, but we can't stay under these covers. I'm suffocating in here."

"You increase the level of difficulty," Ryan smiled, "but I'm up to the challenge. Let's do it."

"My little romantic," Jamie smiled, patting Ryan's cheek fondly.

Tossing the covers back, Ryan took a breath, the cool air filling her lungs. Jamie cuddled up against her side and started to draw little patterns on Ryan's overly-warm body. Caitlin turned over in her sleep, muttering an adorable little bit of gibberish. "She's talking in her sleep," Jamie giggled.

"Awake or asleep, that ain't talking," Ryan whispered as she started to laugh, putting the pillow over her face to keep quiet. When she calmed down she pulled the pillow down just far enough so that Jamie could see her eyes. "I can't do this," she mumbled. "There's no way I can relax enough."

"I can't either," Jamie agreed. "It might be different if she was our child, but it just seems…I don't know…too odd."

"Yeah, that's a good way to put it. Besides, you never know what she takes in while she's asleep. I'd be embarrassed as all get-out to take her back to her parents and have them find out that her first words were …Oh, God."

The next morning, at a little after six, Jamie woke slowly, blinked at the clock, and snuggled closer to her partner, deciding to delay the onset of the new day as long as possible. Surprisingly, something kept her from falling asleep again, and it took her a few minutes to realize what it was. *It's better to stay awake and feel how wonderful it is to be held like this*, she decided. She had no idea how Ryan managed it, but not infrequently Jamie woke to the delicious sensation of being completely enveloped by the strong, smooth arms of her beloved. It was puzzling, since they rarely fell asleep like that, so she just chalked it up to O'Flaherty magic.

She was lying on her side, with Ryan cuddled up tight against her back. Her cheek rested on Ryan's left bicep, her head nestled between soft swells of breast. Ryan's right arm encircled her waist, and her hands were clasped together, seemingly protecting Jamie from all harm. The scents that emanated from Ryan surrounded Jamie like a warm, humid cloud. A little soap, a little baby powder, just a touch of musk, and a smidgen of the aromatic Ryan-ness that was impossible to describe, but altogether intoxicating.

Ryan's moist breath was coming in long, smooth streams, blowing softly over the top of Jamie's head. She could feel a few strands of hair propelled on the breeze that wafted over her, and once again she thanked the gods that Ryan rarely snored. *With as much air as goes through those lungs, she'd wake the dead if she ever did.*

She lifted her right arm and covered Ryan's, wrapping her hand around her partner's clasped ones. For a few minutes she merely observed the marked difference in their skin tones, marveling at the rich, deep burnished color of her partner's skin. Even with her chronic use of sun block, Ryan had darkened up during the summer. *Maybe Ryan's right*, she mused. *Maybe she should just have all of our children. She has such good genes, it seems a shame not to exploit them*. Involuntarily, she thought of her own cousins, aunts, and uncles. *Drug addicts or alcoholics, all,* she thought regretfully. *It doesn't get much better on the Evans side, either. I can look forward to giving birth to a controlling, manipulative philanderer.*

She lifted her hand and started to stroke up and down Ryan's muscular arm, breathing deeply of her scent. *You don't see the O'Flahertys running around with other women. Not one divorce in the entire clan—on either side. That's quite a statement when half of all marriages end in divorce*.

As she snuggled closer, she felt the hard tips of Ryan's nipples rub against her back. Sighing heavily she prayed, *Please, please don't ever cheat on me, baby. I couldn't live without your love.*

Her hand continued to stroke, finally dropping to draw a smooth path from Ryan's hip to her knee, reveling in the feel of her lover's soft skin.

Slowly, Ryan opened her eyes, then grasped the hand and placed a gentle kiss on the warm palm. "Morning, love," she yawned as she immediately went into her stretching routine.

Jamie continued to stroke her all over while she stretched and purred. When the questing hand wandered a little too far into dangerous territory, Ryan gently stopped her with another kiss. "Don't tempt me, baby, you know my resistance is weak. My tank's still empty from last week."

"You know I have needs," she purred, dipping her head to nibble on Ryan's collarbone.

Turning over to face her partner, Ryan gently trailed her fingers over Jamie's face, causing a shiver to run down her spine. "I know all about your needs. You were the one to drive me to distraction last night with those torrid kisses."

"And you were the one who gave me that arousing back rub," she reminded her as she kissed her nose. "Getting me all turned on and then trying to compromise my virtue with an innocent child in the room."

"Wasn't my first choice," Ryan smiled. "You were the one who wouldn't do it on the sofa in the living room."

"My mother was in the next room," Jamie moaned.

"Didn't stop you on Tuesday," Ryan reminded her. "Is the sofa more scandalous than the floor?"

Jamie giggled, thinking that her appropriateness meter did tend to jump around a bit. "No, it's not. I just felt a little uncomfortable doing it with my mom so close. You caught me by surprise on Tuesday, Tiger. It's when I have time to think that I get prudish."

"You're far from prudish." Ryan's large, warm hands were slowly running all over the naked body, and Jamie's libido decided that it needed an outlet.

"Bathroom?" she asked hopefully.

A slow shake of the head was Ryan's answer. "We won't hear Caitlin when she wakes."

"Hallway?"

"Now that has possibilities," Ryan agreed with a growl as she tossed Jamie onto her back and climbed aboard to nuzzle her neck. Jamie's wild giggling woke the baby and after Caitlin had a second to orient herself, she cried to be picked up. "Now aren't you glad you weren't seconds from orgasm?" Ryan asked smugly as she jumped out of bed and lifted the infant from her crib.

"I never thought that was a question I'd say yes to, but I suppose I am," she admitted, flopping back to the bed with a thump.

"Don't worry. We'll be in our snug little bed tonight, and I'll fulfill every fantasy you have."

"Oh, I know you, Ms. O'Flaherty. You'll be so tired tonight you'll have no interest in my aching body."

"I'd have to be a lot more than tired to lose interest in that masterpiece. Comatose, unconscious…" she trailed off as she went into the bath to start the shower.

They were just packing up the last of their supplies when Catherine came popping out of her room, showered, dressed, and ready. "Let's go," she said brightly.

"You want to go with us?" Jamie gaped, having assumed her mother had satisfied all of her amusement park fantasies on her earlier visit.

"Of course I do. It's our last day here, and I want to enjoy myself. I might even go on a ride or two," she declared, grasping Caitlin's stroller and leading the way from the room, her startled companions trailing along behind.

They decided to have breakfast in Goofy's Kitchen, located right in their hotel. Catherine had not experienced the earlier visit with the big dog, so she bubbled with delight as Caitlin greeted her old friend Goofy. The huge dog was standing by the entrance to the restaurant, and an automatic camera caught an adorable picture of the pair, both blondes smiling broadly. Catherine didn't know that her picture had been taken, but Jamie saw the image flash on the monitors over the reception area, and she remained behind to purchase one of the large color photos.

The restaurant, while crowded, was well designed, and it didn't seem as noisy or as packed as it truly was. The fare was served buffet style—never one of Jamie's favorite things, but right up Ryan's alley. Looking around the various serving areas, Jamie nodded her approval. There were quite a number of items designed for kids, such as peanut butter and jelly pizza, but they also stocked many things to appeal to the adult palate. Never liking to eat much in the morning, she grabbed a croissant, some raspberry jam, and an assortment of fresh fruit.

Ryan shot her partner a pleading look, silently complaining that holding Caitlin interfered with her ability to gather enough food for herself. Jamie prepared a plate for her, managing to pile many of Ryan's favorites onto one plate, adding two Mickey shaped waffles when Ryan made eyes at them. They were heading back to the table when the bright blue eyes lit up in glee as Ryan saw the large clear dispensers for various cereals. "Jamie, can we get these for our house?"

Jamie's brow furrowed; there was no way in hell she was going to have four or five massive cereal dispensers on her counter, but she didn't have the heart to disappoint her partner. "Sure, honey," she said, knowing that the idea would flee Ryan's mind by the time they left the restaurant. Taking the biggest bowl she could find, Jamie filled it with one helping from each of the containers, creating a very satisfactory helping of "Ryan's Jumble."

Catherine settled Caitlin onto her lap, insisting that Ryan and Jamie have a moment to enjoy their meal in peace. The baby happily ate from the huge bowl of cereal, repeatedly sticking her chubby little hand into the bowl. They had wisely decided to add milk later, much to Catherine's pleasure, and Ryan began to doubt that there would be any cereal left for her. Caitlin often ate very little, but sometimes her hunger seemed inexhaustible, and this morning was one of those occasions. By the time everyone else was finished with their first helping, the cereal bowl was almost empty, and Cait was looking around for more.

"Boy, some people don't know when to stop," Ryan chided her, receiving dramatically rolled eyes from her partner.

Catherine was in a very perky mood, and with a jolt Jamie realized why. *She hasn't had a drink since we've been here. Not waking up with a hangover for two days has got to be nice.* Before the trip to Rhode Island, Jamie had considered talking to her mother about her drinking, but the upsetting events of that week had made her reconsider bringing up a topic that she knew would be difficult. Seeing her mother abstain for three days made her question her drinking habits. *Could it be that she just drinks because she's bored? It seems like she'd need to drink every day if she was an alcoholic, yet she hasn't even looked for alcohol.* Deciding that she couldn't resolve the question today, Jamie put it into the "for later discussion" pile and tried to focus on the present.

Entering the park, they immediately got in line for the Matterhorn, since they hadn't ridden it the day before. Ryan explained that it was a much tamer ride than Space Mountain, but since it was a landmark they should probably do it. "How do you know so much about these rides if you haven't been here?" Jamie inquired suspiciously.

"There're tons of sites on the net dealing with all things Disney," Ryan said. "These rides aren't really considered coasters by the purists, but I still found out a lot about them the other night when I was surfing."

"I always think you're doing some heady science stuff when you're at your computer. I guess I'd better keep a closer eye on you," she threatened, giving Ryan a narrow-eyed glare.

"Eyes, hands, mouth…you can come closer with any body part you wish."

"Mother will hear you!" Jamie whispered, her eyes wide.

"Over Caitlin's babbling?" Ryan asked, casting a fond glance at the pair. Caitlin was indeed talking loudly, albeit nonsensically, right into Catherine's ear.

"Good point. I'm afraid Mother will have to make an appointment with an audiologist when she gets home."

Catherine and Caitlin waited in line with them after Ryan explained that they could exit through the 'chicken gate' right before she and Jamie boarded. Just before it was their turn, Jamie stood on her tiptoes and whispered something into Ryan's ear. Ryan gave her a little smirk and shrugged her shoulders, showing mild agreement. Reaching out to take the baby, Jamie turned to her mother as she said, "Ryan's going to take you on this one, Mom. Have fun." And with that she scampered out of the chicken gate, leaving a dumbstruck Catherine and a laughing Ryan.

Ryan placed a gentle hand on her shoulder as she assured her, "This one isn't bad, Catherine, but if you don't want to do it, I'm happy to ride alone."

The stunned woman took in a deep breath and steeled herself as she confidently replied, "I'm no chicken." Ryan laughed and patted her soundly on the back as their car pulled up. The little car held only four passengers, two in the front seat and two in the back. Ryan got into the back seat first and Catherine gamely stepped in and settled back against her. She was a little uncomfortable to be sitting between Ryan's long legs, and more than a little scared, but before she could change her mind the bar came down, locking her firmly in place.

"Okay," Ryan said into her ear, her deep, warm voice very reassuring. "This one does a lot of up and down motion, but you're never upside down. Just try to relax and let your body move with the car." Catherine was sitting so rigidly that Ryan was afraid she would snap in half once the ride started. "Would you like me to hold you?" she asked, her warm breath strangely reassuring.

The frightened woman shook her head, not wanting to appear helpless in front of Ryan. "I'm okay," she muttered, her voice sounding high and tight even to her own ears.

The car pulled away and immediately began a rather steep ascent. Gravity thrust her back against Ryan's chest, which should have embarrassed her, but strangely, she found that it comforted her. Ryan felt so sturdy and soft and warm that she somehow felt mothered, even though her mother had been none of those things.

Their little car reached the crest of the hill and as they started to tumble over, Catherine grabbed Ryan's arms from the sides of the car and flung them across her chest, not even bothering to be embarrassed by the gentle laugh that bubbled up from the amused woman.

Her hands grabbed onto Ryan's forearms as they flew down the side of the mountain. The little car zigged and zagged as it turned and banked and dipped. She held on tighter as the ride continued to bounce and spin, holding her captive just a bit longer than she wished. Finally, they flew past a small waterfall that sprinkled them lightly as they drew to a smooth stop.

Catherine let out a breath as the bar lifted and they were allowed to depart. Ryan waited for a moment, then another, looking up at the attendant who was giving them a wry smile. Leaning over, she softly reminded Catherine, "You can let go now."

Pulled from her daze, Catherine barked out a laugh as she immediately released her death grip on Ryan's arms. "I'm so sorry, Ryan, but I just had to hold on. I thought I was going to fly out of that little car, and if I did I was taking you with me!"

Ryan slid an arm around her shoulders as she escorted her out to an expectantly waiting pair of blondes. "Was it fun?" Jamie asked excitedly.

Caitlin held out her arms to Catherine who gladly claimed her. As they walked along she kept repeating, "Fun. Was it fun?"

They were a good 50 yards down the path when she finally turned to Jamie and said decisively, "Yes, it *was* fun. It was enough fun to last a lifetime."

The next stop was Fantasyland, and on the way Catherine caught a glimpse of the vivid red fingerprints on Ryan's forearms. "My God, Ryan, I've hurt you!"

"Nah, I won't even bruise," she said. "You just put a little pressure on my skin. It'll be gone soon."

"Goodness," Catherine cried, "I swear I haven't grabbed anyone that hard since I gave birth to Jamie."

Never having heard the story of her birth, Jamie ventured to ask, "Was Daddy with you?"

"Oh, yes, for part of the time."

Must have had to leave for a hot date, Jamie groused to herself, her image of her father now intrinsically melded with another woman.

Ryan was still able to converse about Jim in a normal fashion, so she asked the follow-up. "Just part of the time?"

"Yes, they finally asked him to leave," she said. "There's something about the sound of your husband retching that makes labor even less pleasant."

She gave Ryan an amused smile, showing that it didn't bother her to talk about it, so Ryan asked, "Was that when you were about to deliver?"

"No, dear," Catherine said lightly. "It was when the doctor came in to examine me just after we got into a labor room."

"How long were you in labor?"

"Close to a full day…around 20 hours."

"And when did Jim leave?"

"Around 20 minutes," Catherine smirked. "He tried to come in several more times, but he was more distracting than helpful, so I banished him."

Jamie had been listening intently, unable to keep a smile off her face. She knew in her soul that if she ever gave birth, her partner would be right by her side, no matter what.

"Don't go getting any ideas, Jamie," Ryan warned, not as confident of her partner's constitution. "Only men can get away with that ploy."

Ryan was dying to ride the teacups, and she had been reminding them of that fact ever since they had first ventured into the park. Jamie was willing to wait in line with her, but she refused to get on, knowing that Ryan's need for speed was tremendously greater than her own. Even though she trusted her partner with her life, she wasn't sure that she trusted her with her stomach, so she begged off.

Ryan finally convinced the others to join her by pledging that she would let either Jamie or Catherine turn the wheel that imparted the spin. The baby was able to go on this ride, and Ryan knew she would have a blast. The line was still very short since most people didn't like the "spin 'n barfs" this early in the day. Caitlin was in her baby sling, and Ryan moved it from her back to her chest so that the baby was nestled between her thighs when she sat down. When the ride was full, they began the slow lazy spin. Caitlin looked around suspiciously but when she saw that everyone else was having fun, she decided she might as well have fun too. The ride picked up speed until it was going at quite a little clip, just fast enough for a nice sensation. Once Caitlin got used to the motion, she wanted more. She jumped up and down forcefully, screaming in delight as her short golden hair whipped around her head.

Ryan taunted Jamie, who was in charge of the wheel, "Spin it! Come on, spin it!" She reluctantly complied, giving the wheel a tiny turn, barely enough to turn the car a half revolution. Ryan scoffed at her but smiled widely, honoring her promise not to interfere. When the ride slowed to a stop, Ryan convinced the young attendant to allow her to take another spin. He complied since there weren't enough people waiting to fill it, and she was lucky enough to be able to ride solo.

As the ride began, Jamie saw the demonic look in her partner's eye and warned her mother, "I think Buffy is going to make an appearance."

"Pardon?" Catherine asked.

"That's what I call her wild child. Look at her eyes."

Catherine did as she was told, and was a bit amazed at the transformation. Ryan looked like a feral animal as she turned the wheel faster and faster. She pounded on the wheel until her arms grew tired, then she immediately turned it the other way as fast as she could pump. Her hair blew around wildly as she threw her head back and laughed. Other people were having fun, too, but no one looked as happy as Ryan. When the ride finally came to a stop the young attendant sidled up to her cup and asked, "Go again?"

"All day," Ryan scoffed, hoping that one more time was all she got. She repeated her actions, which resulted in the totally dizzy, disoriented feeling that she truly loved. When the third trip was over, she hopped out quickly but walked right into the metal gate that surrounded the ride. Jamie made eye contact with the smirking operator, who allowed her to come in through the exit and lead her stumbling partner to safety.

"That was so much fun!" Ryan cried, clinging to Jamie as the park spun wildly around her. "And it's the longest ride here, 'cause it's still going," she said giddily.

Chapter Six

They managed both the Thunder Mountain and Indiana Jones rides before the park started to fill up. It was nearly lunchtime and Caitlin was starting to get a little fussy, so they decided to go back to the room for a nap. After feeding her a half jar of tapioca, Ryan placed the baby in the crib and sang to her while Jamie and Catherine relaxed in the living room.

"You're not mad at me for tricking you into going on the Matterhorn, are you?" Jamie asked.

"Of course not. I'm glad I went."

"Was it scary?"

"At first it was," she reflected. "But I have to admit that having Ryan holding on to me made me feel strangely comforted."

"That's how I feel when she holds me. I feel warm and safe and impervious to harm. There's just no safer place on earth."

Ryan came out as they were talking, and sat on the opposite end of the sofa from her partner. Jamie immediately lifted her legs and tossed them onto Ryan's lap. "Foot rub?" she begged. Ryan gave her a gentle smile as she did her bidding without question.

"So what do you want to do for the rest of the day?" Catherine asked. "We need to leave for the airport by 5:30 since we have to arrive by seven. I assume we'll need to have dinner before that, since we won't get in to the city until 9:30 and I know Ryan can't wait that late to eat," Catherine smiled, knowing her daughter-in-law's habits already.

"I know what Caitlin wants to do," Ryan observed, "but I wanna do the boat races again." She had a childlike grin on her face, and Catherine cocked her head in question.

"Boat races?"

Jamie rolled her eyes and said, "They have a little pond by the restaurant we ate at on Tuesday. Didn't you notice it?"

"No, I don't think so."

"Well, Ryan doesn't miss a thing, and she noticed that one of the boats was named Ronewa Ryan, whatever that means. You control the boat with these big steering wheels, and you can take it around the little pond and dock it next to an island. I haven't been able to get her away from them since." She gave her partner a fond smile and said, "For someone who hates to waste money, you sure were tossing your quarters into that game."

"It was like the kind of video games they had out when I was a kid," Ryan insisted. "But it was real. Well, kinda real," she admitted sheepishly.

"Other than playing your game what would you two like to do?" Catherine asked.

"I don't really have anything on my agenda," Ryan said. "How about you, honey?"

"What about a workout? You haven't done much since we've been here. There is a small fitness center in the hotel. Would you like to use it?"

"No. I think I can satisfy both Caitlin and myself by going to the pool."

After a room service lunch, Catherine arranged for a late checkout, and they made their way down to the pool. When they arrived, Ryan went to speak with the lifeguard, who directed her to a large storage bin on the end of the pool deck. She came back with a wide blue belt, explaining that it was a jogging belt which would help her stay buoyant while she "ran" in the deep water.

They all hopped in the water, Catherine and Jamie staying in the shallow end with the baby, Ryan going to the deep end. She began to bob up and down in the water, moving along rather quickly. Jamie watched her as she developed a rhythm and began to ignore everything around her. She could tell that Ryan was getting into one of her zones and she just glanced at her occasionally to check on her progress over the next hour. Caitlin didn't mind her absence since she could see her, so everyone was happy.

After a solid hour of exercise Ryan came back over looking a little winded. "That's a lot of fun," she said happily. "It's nice to get the strain off my knees once in a while."

Given that Ryan claimed to be interested in guarding her knees, her next activity seemed an odd choice. She carried a pair of sand-filled dumbbells to the five-foot depth and began to do a strange exercise that Jamie assumed she had just devised. She crouched down as low as she could go, assisted by the weights. Then she would burst from the water and leap as high as she could go. She repeated this at least 100 times, and both Evans women grew tired just watching her. But young Caitlin grew more animated by the minute. By the time Ryan was finished, the baby was slapping the water with both arms and jumping up and down as well as she could with her unsteady legs.

To her great delight, Ryan came over and snatched her up, holding her above her head until they were back in the five-foot depth. This time, instead of the weights, Ryan held Caitlin. She was light for her age; nonetheless, she weighed in at around 20 pounds. Ryan extended her arms fully and locked her elbows. Again she launched into a deep squat, but she kept her eyes on the baby as she submerged. When Caitlin was in the water just to her waist, Ryan shot up again, pushing the baby high into the air, much to her squealing amusement.

Catherine and Jamie watched the proceedings in fascination, as did most of the other guests. Caitlin was nearly hysterical with glee, and she giggled and shrieked nonstop. Ryan stopped frequently to make sure she was enjoying herself, but with even a momentary pause the baby jumped and stretched, trying to imitate the movement.

The game went on four times longer than Jamie imagined it could, and by the time Ryan slogged over to them she was completely out of breath. She handed Caitlin over to Catherine and flopped onto her back while Jamie lent a hand to augment her buoyancy. "She's insatiable!" Ryan finally gasped out with a laugh.

"Gee, I wonder where she gets it from," Jamie dryly remarked.

"Hey, we only share one quarter of the same gene pool," she protested.

"Maybe so, but some of this is environmental, and all of that is from you and Conor."

Catherine was still in shock from watching Ryan work nonstop the entire time they had been at the pool. "Do you always play this hard?" she asked.

"No, but I've got to get in shape for volleyball."

"Could I come to see some of your games?" Catherine asked. "I don't think I've ever been to a volleyball match."

"Sure. You can come and sit in the O'Flaherty rooting section. When I played sports at USF I usually accounted for half of the crowd."

"You're going to have to give both of us some instructions, Ryan," Jamie reminded her. "I've only seen volleyball played at the beach, and I think your collegiate game is a lot different than that."

"Yes and no. The strategy is a lot different, and there are a ton of different rules, but the concept is the same—hit it where they ain't!"

To cool down, Ryan took the baby on the long water slide a few dozen times. Jamie had warned her that Caitlin would not be able to stop once they started, but Ryan was just headstrong enough to ignore her warnings. As expected, when five o'clock rolled around, the baby was still going strong and very upset about leaving such a wonderful place. Luckily, the crying spell was much shorter than the day before, likely because she was totally exhausted. After five minutes of weak sobs, she fell asleep, and remained so while the adults quickly showered and changed.

They had packed earlier, and when the bellman showed up to take their bags, Jamie caught her partner struggling to put every piece of fruit and cheese from the gift basket into her suitcase. She caught Jamie watching her and gave an embarrassed giggle. "I can't bear to waste good food," she admitted.

"I think it's an adorable trait," Jamie replied, giving her a healthy squeeze.

On the way down in the elevator, Caitlin woke briefly, managing to stay alert until they were settled in the limo. As her last conscious act, she followed Ryan's instructions, waving goodbye to Mickey as they pulled away.

Since they were making good time through Orange County, Ryan checked her watch and said, "Can we stop for a little dinner? I'm weak with the hunger."

"Of course, dear," Catherine agreed. "Just tell the driver what you want. I'm sure he knows where things are."

A half hour later, Ryan crushed the wrapper from her In-N-Out Double-Double, and sighed, "This is living large." After a moment of reflection she turned to Catherine and said, "Other than the AIDS Ride and visits to my family in Ireland, this is the first vacation I've ever had. I think it's obvious how much I've enjoyed myself, Catherine. I just can't thank you enough." Her beaming smile was infectious and Catherine returned it happily.

"The pleasure was truly mine. I can't remember having more fun than I've had these last three days. I felt like a kid again or, should I say, for the first time."

When they reached the airport it was 7:10 and Ryan looked around in dismay at the mess they had created in the back of the limo. But when she saw the tip that Catherine handed the driver her guilt was immediately assuaged. *He could have the thing detailed with that amount,* she thought wryly. *That's one more thing I've got to say for Catherine: she knows how to tip.*

By the time they got everything checked and made a stop in the spacious bathroom to change the baby, they were called to board. The flight was only half full and only had one other passenger in first class. The flight attendant came by to introduce himself as they were getting settled. "Hi, I'm Robert," he said in a friendly fashion. "Looks like you've got me almost to yourselves, so if you need anything at all, please call. I get lonely back there all by myself."

"We could use a bottle warmed," Catherine said.

"Be back in a jiffy," he said after Catherine instructed him on how to do it properly.

When he returned, he spent a few minutes inquiring about the baby. When he asked if they lived in San Francisco, Ryan piped up, "My partner and I live in the city. Upper Noe. But her mother," here she pointed out Catherine, "lives down in the Peninsula."

He stood with his hands on his hips and slapped Ryan on the shoulder playfully. "That gorgeous young creature is not your mother-in-law. Don't even go there!"

Catherine grinned broadly as she replied, "Guilty as charged."

"You must have been nine when you had her." He turned to Jamie and said, "Although you could be 14..."

"Hey, I'm 21," she said with a touch of pique.

"I've got ties older than you are, sweetie," he chided her. As he turned back to Catherine he said conspiratorially, "I think it's fabulous that you have a new baby. You go, girl!"

Catherine blushed but did not correct him. She merely got Caitlin settled in her car seat and began to feed her the bottle as Robert went to tend to his other passenger.

They took off a few minutes late, but once again they didn't have to wait long for clearance. The baby was more aware this time, but to everyone's relief, she seemed much more interested than frightened. After they had been in the air 15 minutes or so she fell asleep, and shortly afterwards Catherine joined her. Ryan was so charmed by the sight of Catherine's blonde head resting on the top of the car seat that she insisted that Jamie get up and snap a picture.

The young women sat close together in the big leather seats, holding hands and snuggling a little, both starting to relax from the very hectic day. Robert just grinned at them each time he passed, but after a little while he didn't reappear for a long while. Ryan gave Jamie a sly little grin as she dipped her head and began to plant tiny kisses all the way along the ridge of her jaw line.

Jamie was a little hesitant, but after a moment she gave in and tilted her head back to allow her lover full access. Ryan continued her assault, dipping down to her exposed collarbones and the hollow between them. Jamie's hands lifted involuntarily as she threaded her fingers through the dark hair and grasped Ryan's head tenderly, pressing it to her sensitized neck as she let out a soft moan.

Getting a verbal reaction always compelled Ryan to go further, and she moved from the soft neck on to the even softer ears. Jamie's toes curled when the warm, wet mouth claimed her always-sensitive ear, shivers chasing down her spine while Ryan's tongue softly teased every bit of skin.

Sighing deeply, Jamie lifted her lover's head and gazed into her vivid blue eyes. "You're playing with fire, baby," she warned, her voice low and languid. "I'm not sure you want Mother to wake up and see your pants around your ankles."

"I'm just trying to eliminate some foreplay later tonight," Ryan said innocently. "I like to make good use of down time."

Her head dipped to return to Jamie's ear, but Jamie pulled her face close and rewarded her with a scorching kiss that sent chills running down Ryan's spine to slam into her groin. She let out a breath as though she had been punched, as Jamie smiled sweetly and patted her cheek. "Two can play your little game, Ryan. Don't underestimate your opponent." With that, she tossed her hair and crawled over her stunned partner to make use of the restroom.

A few minutes later Jamie opened the restroom door to exit. She looked up in shock as a warm hand made contact with her chest and firmly pushed her back in. Ryan's eyes burned into hers as Buffy made her second appearance of the trip. Jamie gulped audibly when she saw the fire in those crystal eyes and she knew that no matter what her brain told her, it would be overridden by her hungry body. She felt herself being lifted and placed onto the sink as Ryan slid between her open legs. Her head was tilted up by Ryan's gentle fingers, and she soon felt all of her concerns fly from her mind as those incredibly soft lips captured hers, and her racing mind calming as her body was enfolded into Ryan's warm embrace.

Twenty minutes later Jamie slid out of the bathroom and spent a moment straightening her clothing. *Thank goodness I wore a dress*, she mused as she ran her fingers through her hair. *Now I just have to wipe the smile from my face.*

To her eternal gratitude, both of their companions were still sleeping peacefully when she slid back into her seat. Several minutes later, Ryan joined her and gently pinned something to her dress just over her breast. "What's this?" Jamie asked as she looked down.

"Your wings," her lover explained with a grin. "This means you're now a member of the Mile High Club. Robert gave them to me with his congratulations."

The flush traveled from her chest to her hairline in record time. "You told him?"

"Well, sure," Ryan replied logically. "I had to submit your name to headquarters."

Jamie looked at her as though she had lost her mind, but Ryan's poker face finally gave way to a hearty laugh. "I asked him for some wings for Caitlin to commemorate her first trip," she explained, "but the look on your face was worth walking back home from L.A."

"You're gonna be walking," Jamie threatened as she narrowed her eyes. "Actually I might just toss you out from here."

"And not ten minutes ago you were singing, or should I say howling, my praises," she scoffed. "You sure are mercurial."

Jamie dropped her head onto Ryan's broad shoulder as she enthused, "Don't ever change, Ryan O'Flaherty. You're absolutely perfect just the way you are."

As arranged, Tommy and Annie were waiting for them at the gate with anxious, wide-eyed looks on their smiling faces. Three of the four travelers were very happy to see them, but Caitlin was absolutely uninterested. She turned sharply and buried her head into Catherine's chest as Annie ran over to the foursome to claim her precious one. Her face fell when she realized that Caitlin was shunning her, and Ryan knew that tears were just a heartbeat away, so she tried to mediate the issue after a quick introduction of all the parties. "Let's go over to Starbucks and have some cocoa," she suggested pointing out the omnipresent coffee bar just a few dozen feet away.

As they walked along, Catherine continued to carry the baby. "I can't tell you how precious she was during the entire trip," she reassured them. "She loved the plane and she slept perfectly. She was an absolute angel."

Both Annie and Tommy smiled at the compliments, but it was clear that they were heartbroken by Caitlin's snubbing. When they entered the coffee shop, Jamie took everyone's order and went with Ryan to fetch the beverages. Tommy grabbed enough chairs for all, and Catherine sat down, still holding the baby snuggled into her chest.

Looking at Tommy and Annie with compassion, she revealed, "The exact same thing happened to me when Jamie was a baby. Regrettably, rather than just a few days, I was gone for two weeks when she was about 16 months old." She smiled sadly at the memory as she continued. "I don't know how much you know about Jamie's youth, but she was raised much more by her nanny that she was by me." Tommy and Annie nodded, even though they had not known this fact about their friend.

"The nanny assured me that it wouldn't be too traumatic for her, so I went on my usual summer trip to Italy and left her at home with her father and her nanny. I hadn't been gone more than two days before I realized what a mistake I'd made, but when I called home they assured me that everything was fine. In a way, it was, and Jamie did just fine without me, but when I got home, she acted like she had never seen me before in her life. She'd learned a dozen new words, and she was taller and heavier—she was like a different child."

Jamie and Ryan came back to the table just then. They could tell that Catherine was recounting a story, so they slipped quietly into their chairs. "One of the worst mistakes of my parenting career was not the fact that I left her—I think she would have quickly forgiven me for that. But once I came back, I know that I shied away from her. It hurt me so much to have her ignore me that I just withdrew even further from her life. I allowed her nanny to have an even bigger role in her upbringing, which was a grave mistake that I will never forgive myself for." Jamie slid her arm around her mother's shoulders, showing that she had fully forgiven her. Catherine smiled warmly at her daughter, blinking back a few tears as she said, "I'm sure Caitlin will get over being angry with you as soon as she gets home. But please try not to be angry with her for feeling a little abandoned."

Tears were falling down Annie's cheeks as Catherine finished her story. Jamie was crying as well, and after sucking in a ragged breath, Catherine joined her. Annie started to sob in earnest as she saw everyone else in the same state.

The baby knew that something was going on, and she warily lifted her head from Catherine's chest and cast a tentative look up. She paused for a moment, seeing both Catherine and Jamie crying, then she turned quickly, seeking out her mother. When she saw her sobbing, she burst into tears, twisting her little body as she held her arms out to her mother. “Mama!” she cried to force her attention. Annie looked up and caught sight of those big green eyes as another flood of tears overcame her. She reached out for the baby as Catherine leaned forward to deliver her. Caitlin collapsed onto Annie’s chest, crying softly and muttering, “Mama, Mama,” repeatedly, her little voice strangled with emotion.

There was not a dry eye in the group by this time, with even Tommy surreptitiously wiping his eyes. Caitlin continued to stand on Annie’s legs and hug her, allowing both of her parents to comfort her. Jamie had wrapped her arm around her mother and was giving her a well deserved hug, very proud of her for sharing such a painful story. Only Ryan was left out, so she snuck her hand under the table to gently grasp Jamie’s thigh.

“Well, that’s not how I expected her first words to come, but they were sure welcome!” Annie gushed when she was composed again.

“That was her first word?” Catherine asked. “Jamie, get your camera. We need to record this moment.”

Jamie pulled her camera from her bag and snapped a few pictures of a now beaming Annie and Tommy with their happy, verbal child.

“Don’t worry, Tommy,” Ryan said knowledgeably. “I have a feeling that Dada is right around the corner.”

“I’m not worried,” he smiled, still fighting for composure. “If that’s the only word she ever says, I’ll be happy.”

When everyone had dried their eyes, Catherine asked, “Back to work tomorrow, Tommy?”

“After a fashion. Our house is a rental, and the landlord’s been after us to have the house exterminated. We decided this was a perfect time, so we let him do it while we were gone. We’re going to spend the next couple of days cleaning the place so it's safe for the baby."

"That certainly doesn't sound like much fun," Catherine said solicitously. "What will you do with her?"

"We'll take turns watching her over at my mother's house. We can't have her near the place until we're sure it's safe."

Jamie leaned over and whispered something to her mother and then to her lover. She obviously got two affirmative responses because she quickly made her offer. "I propose you go back to Pebble Beach and get some bonding time in with Caitlin. If you spend three days playing with her in the pool, I guarantee all will be forgiven."

"But Jamie, we can't do that!" Annie protested. "Your parents want their house back for the weekend, and we've got to clean."

"I don't want the house back for the weekend," Catherine assured them. "I'm going to pack up and head off to Italy, so the house will be empty. I'd love for you to return to the beach."

"Ryan and I will recruit the rest of the family to help us clean your house," Jamie added. "If we get everybody over on Saturday, we can be done in a few hours. Please let us help you out. I really think Caitlin needs your undivided attention for a little while."

Tommy looked at Annie for just a moment before saying, "You've got a deal. I don't know how we'll ever repay any of you, but I think Caitie does need some attention, and her needs come first."

"Speaking of attention," Annie said brightly, "which one of you gave her this fantastic haircut?" She ran her fingers through the pale blonde hair that attractively framed her little round face.

"Neither of us," Jamie admitted. "We took her with us when we got our hair cut on Monday. The fellow who cuts our hair is crazy for babies, and they both had a ball. I think we have to keep taking her there."

"Okay," Annie agreed, "But you have to let us pay for her haircuts. We can't keep imposing on you like that."

"Be careful what you ask for," Ryan said mysteriously. "You may get it."

After many tears were shed, they all said their goodbyes. Tommy and Annie insisted on taking Catherine home, and she happily agreed. "I get to spend a few more minutes with my little Cupcake," she whispered to Jamie as they hugged goodbye. She held Jamie out at arm's length and said, "I'm sorry that I didn't take you to Disneyland 20 years ago, but I'm so glad that you let me take you now."

"I know I had a better time than I would have 20 years ago," Jamie said, meaning every word. "Thanks for taking us."

Ryan came over and extended her arms, smiling when the older woman gave her the usual light kisses on the cheek. She waited until Catherine started to pull away, then wrapped her in her arms, resting her chin on top of her head as they hugged gently. "I hope you don't mind, but I can't stand those dainty little kisses. In my family we touch when we hug," she chuckled.

Catherine sighed, feeling her body relax into the warm embrace. "I could grow to like this, Ryan," she murmured into the soft cotton of the tall young woman's blouse.

"That's my plan," she admitted, releasing her with a little pat. Grinning down at her mother-in-law, Ryan said, "Thanks for everything, Catherine. I hope this was the first of many trips we'll take together."

"You'd be on Alitalia with me on Saturday if you'd say yes. I guarantee many, many future adventures, Ryan."

They snatched Caitlin away for a group hug as they each kissed her little blonde head. When she was returned to Tommy's firm hold she snuggled her head down onto his chest and sleepily batted her eyes at her baby-sitters. Upon cue, she waved bye-bye as they parted ways, peeking over her father's shoulder for one last look as the groups took off in different directions.

As the elevator transported them to their car, they leaned heavily against each other and the walls of the elevator. "I could sleep for a week," Ryan moaned.

"I could stay in bed for a week," Jamie purred as she stole a kiss.

"You have become my insatiable love nymph," Ryan chided her in a teasing tone. "What am I going to do with you?"

"Whatever you want," she promised. "As long as you start tonight."

"No one's here," Ryan marveled as they walked into the O'Flaherty home. "I mean no one. Not even Duffy."

"Here's a note," Jamie said, finding a pad on the dining table with a message in Martin's neat hand. Reading it quickly she informed Ryan, "Your father says he's taking Duffy out for his usual lengthy walk." Her face crinkled up into a grin as she said, "I think that's code for the fact that he's with your aunt."

"Yeah, Duffy's getting a good deal out of this clandestine courtship. He not only gets to go on long walks with the two of them, he also gets to hang out at Aunt Maeve's in the evenings. He loves it over there," she laughed. "He can usually find cookie remnants from Caitlin hidden somewhere."

"It's only nine thirty," Jamie said. "Wanna stay upstairs and wait for him to get home so we can tell him all about the trip?"

"Yeah," Ryan said excitedly. "That's a great idea. We can stay up for hours and hours…talking about every little detail. Then we can go downstairs and collapse before our heads hit the pillow. Good thinking!"

Placing her hands on her hips, Jamie stared at her and said, "Ryan O'Flaherty—I think you're making fun of me."

Wrapping her up in a tender hug Ryan said, "Not you, honey. Just your idea. I have one thing...and one thing only on my agenda...and it doesn't involve talking to my father or petting my dog, even though I love them both. I made you a promise this morning, and I'm gonna keep it."

"Let's see," Jamie said thoughtfully. "A promise...do I remember a promise?"

She tapped at her chin, finally nodding as she said, "That's right. I remember a promise about you making love to me all night long. Is that the promise you're speaking of?"

"That's the one," Ryan agreed, her eyes bright with interest.

"But, honey," Jamie complained, pointing to her chest, "I've got my wings right here. You already pleased me thoroughly. Consider your promise fulfilled." She was clearly teasing as she struggled to keep her grin hidden.

"I had a nice time on the plane, too," Ryan agreed, her eyes roaming up and down Jamie's body like a hungry wolf's. "But that was a very small space, and I'm a very large woman." She was advancing as she spoke and when Jamie felt the dining table hit the backs of her thighs, she linked her hands behind Ryan's neck and smiled up at her. "My needs...my most pressing needs...were unfulfilled," she said, her eyes now glittering with desire.

Maintaining her gaze, Jamie started to stroke her partner gently, starting at her shoulders and traveling down her arms, then her sides, and finally slipping down to her thighs. "Hmm, I don't remember making a promise to make love to you all night long. I distinctly remember that it was a selfless act on your part."

"It was that," Ryan said, leaning closer and closer. She was less than an inch from Jamie's mouth as she said, "You're under no obligation whatsoever, but I can't tell you how much I'd appreciate a little attention. You got my motor running awfully early today, and that little interlude on the plane had me throbbing so badly I was weak-kneed. Have you no sympathy for a poor woman who's just trying to get a little love?"

"Sympathy?" Jamie repeated thoughtfully, stopping to lick playfully at the outline of Ryan's lips. "I wouldn't say that my feelings could be characterized as sympathetic."

"How would you characterize them?" Ryan asked, her voice gone husky with longing. She licked her lips slowly, hoping to entice her lover to bestow a little attention upon them once again.

Catching the not-so-subtle clue, Jamie closed her eyes and let her tongue slip from her lips to tease Ryan mercilessly. Ryan let out a low growl, and Jamie regretfully pulled away to answer her question. "I'd say that my feelings could best be considered erotic…perhaps even wanton," she decided, a sexy grin stealing over her features. "I didn't specifically promise to love you tonight, sweetheart, but worry not. I have the most pleasant obligation imaginable. I made a solemn vow to fulfill every one of your needs for the rest of my life." She wrapped her arms tightly around Ryan's body as she whispered, "Let me fill your…need. In any way that pleases you." The deep, throaty growl and the lascivious look on her face turned Ryan's legs to rubber, and she had to grasp the dining table to keep her balance.

Jamie grabbed her hand and tugged her towards the stairs, smiling when she felt Ryan stumble a bit. *Oh, she's in quite a state*, she smirked to herself. *She's at the peak of arousal when she's not only slow-witted, but ungainly*.

Locking the door immediately, Jamie set about undressing her partner, quickly stripping her out of her Hawaiian shirt and shorts. "I love summer," she said wistfully. "It's so easy to get you naked."

Quirking a smile, Ryan reached out with trembling hands to return the favor, but her progress was abruptly stopped. "Unh-uh," Jamie said decisively. "You don't need to do a thing except relax and enjoy."

"Oh…" Ryan sighed, her eyes wide with gratitude. "You know just what I need…every time."

"I'm glad this is what you need," Jamie said as she pushed her onto the bed. "Because it's definitely what I need." She turned and squatted down a little, presenting her back to her partner. "Pull," she instructed, indicating her zipper.

Ryan did so and tried to stop herself from drooling as she watched the small print dress fall from her partner's shoulders. Constructed in such a way as to negate the need to wear a bra, the falling dress revealed only a lacy white thong, devastatingly sexy on Jamie's fit body.

She left the tiny garment on, since Ryan was particularly fond of thongs, and climbed on top of her. As usual, Ryan's strong hands went to her favorite spot, the bare cheeks that peeked out of the lacy white material. "Do you have any particular requests?" Jamie asked lightly. "Because I have a burning need to do something that's been on my mind since Sunday." She molded her body to Ryan's, her face just a few inches above her partner's moist lips. "I've thought about this every day, sometimes several times a day. Do you know what I've thought about, Ryan? Hmm?"

The dark head shook, Ryan's body thrumming with desire, her brain largely performing only routine maintenance functions as it prepared for the sensual onslaught.

"I've been dreaming of being able to taste you," she said with the sexiest tone of voice that Ryan had ever heard. "I think about how you taste and how you smell, and it just makes me wet." She captured Ryan's open lips in a bruising kiss, her body squirming against her taller partner's as a burst of sensation traveled down her spine. "Does that make you wet, too, Ryan?" she asked with the lethal combination of innocence and lust that drove Ryan absolutely wild.

Ryan knew that her head was nodding, but she wasn't sure she was the one nodding it.

Jamie started to move down the long body, not pausing long enough to kiss or touch any particular part, so intent was she in reaching her target. Her eyes were locked onto Ryan's, the hunger she had for her plainly visible in her fervid gaze. As her head hovered over her goal, Ryan sat up just enough to be able to maintain eye contact, putting a great deal of strain on her abdominal muscles. She still felt as though she was only partially in control of her movements, but something compelled her to summon the strength to support herself in order to see the look on Jamie's face as she first tasted her.

She wasn't disappointed when Jamie's head dipped just enough to allow the warm, pink tongue to slip from her mouth and trail a gentle path straight up the center of her desire. Ryan's mouth opened as her head fell back against her shoulders, but no sound came out. Jamie dipped her head again and again, laving every bit of slick skin with just the tip of her tongue.

After several more charged moments Ryan let out the breath that she had been holding, the force of her exhalation nearly ruffling Jamie's hair. Her body sank back against the mattress, her senses too overloaded to be able to tolerate watching Jamie love her so determinedly.

Ryan was hurtling along at a much faster rate of speed than she wished for, but she knew that she had absolutely no choice in the matter. She wasn't sure when her hands went to Jamie's head and cradled it gently, but soon she was guiding Jamie's head firmly, her hips pumping rhythmically as the silky tongue slipped across her throbbing skin.

Her climax washed over her body, seemingly starting at her toes and flying up to hit her hard, making her cry out loudly as she thrashed about wildly, holding onto Jamie's head with all of her strength.

When the sensation began to ebb, she consciously willed her hands to release and begged, "Hold me?"

In a heartbeat Jamie was cuddled up next to her, holding her tightly while the spasms raced through her long form. Ryan continued to shudder strongly for a few minutes, her body so over-stimulated that Jamie was careful not to move an inch.

Slowly, inexorably, she calmed, finally spreading her arms and legs out to avoid cramping. "Good Lord," she moaned softly. "I felt like I was on Space Mountain again. I was just along for the ride that time. No control whatsoever."

"Mmm," Jamie purred, "you did seem to enjoy yourself."

"That's not even in the ball park," Ryan sighed. "And as soon as I get my brain back I'm gonna think of the proper word to compliment your skills."

Jamie pulled up and smiled at her, pleased with the obvious satisfaction that Ryan had experienced. "That was fun," she said, a silly grin on her face.

"It was indeed," Ryan agreed. "A good time was had by all."

Resting her head against Ryan's chest, feeling the steady, slow beat of her heart, she said, "That's how I feel about our trip. A good time was had by all."

"Mmm-hmm," Ryan agreed, as she began to stretch languidly. "I had a marvelous time."

"It was really nice to get a feel for what it's like to have a child, too, don't you think?"

"I do. I learned a lot."

"Still wanna have a baby?" Jamie asked, turning her head so that she could look into Ryan's eyes.

"Absolutely," Ryan agreed, smiling gently. "I loved caring for Caitlin with you. I feel more than ever that you'll be a fantastic mother. I can't wait," she said wistfully.

"Do you mean that?"

"Mean what?" Ryan asked blankly.

"That you can't wait? I thought you wanted to wait a while..."

"Oh! No, no. That's just an expression. I can wait...I want to wait," she said, her eyes wide with alarm.

Jamie smiled at her and said, "I want to wait, too." She rolled over until she was lying mostly between Ryan's long legs, her chin resting on her hands. "How long do you want to wait?" she asked, crinkling up her nose in an expression that Ryan found adorable.

"I want to wait until my desire for a baby is greater than my desire to spend every possible moment alone with you. I'm far too focused on you to even consider sharing you." With a loving look at her partner Ryan said, "This time is precious. Eventually we have to come down from the clouds and realize there's a world around us." Jamie laughed gently at her exaggeration, but nodded to urge her to continue. "Until that time comes I want my life to revolve around you. You're my sun, and I don't want to share your glorious rays with another soul. I want to be the only planet in your solar system."

Jamie's smiled dimmed and she grew thoughtful, finally saying, "I learned some things on this vacation that really made me think, Ryan. One of the most important things I learned is that there's no greater gift you can give a child than to love her other parent with all of your heart. Before we bring a child into the world, I want to make sure our relationship is rock-solid."

"I agree," Ryan smiled. "Although I think we're pretty solid right now."

"We are," Jamie agreed, nodding as much as her position would allow. "But I feel selfish, too. My heart belongs to you right now. Only you. Someday I'll be ready to share you, but for right now I want to savor you like a fine wine…one delicious sip at a time."

"Beautifully put," Ryan sighed. "Let's make up for lost time and spend the rest of the evening savoring each other."

"Oh, what modest goals you have," Jamie teased. "We're going to spend the rest of our lives savoring each other, Ryan."

Ryan gazed at her partner, her eyes filled with love. She brushed the fine hair from her forehead, smoothing it back gently. "Forever, Jamie," she promised, her voice a mere whisper. "Forever begins tonight."

The End

Author Website
www.susanxmeagher.com

Publisher Website
www.briskpress.com